Look for other Adventure & Western novels
by Eric H. Heisner

West to Bravo

T.H. Elkman

Short Western Tales: Friend of the Devil

Wings of the Pirate

Follow book releases and film productions at:
www.leandogproductions.com

AFRICA TUSK

Eric H. Heisner

Illustrations by Ethan Pro

Dedication

Grandfathers: The men who are always heroes in a young child's heart.

Special Thanks

Travis Eller, Ethan Pro, Dan Farnam
Amber Word Heisner, Clint Beach,
Gena K. Pavey, & Phil Spangenberger:
for his helpful suggestions and advice.

Deep within the Dark Continent of Africa, the dwindling population of wild Elephants is protected by law yet systematically harvested by poachers. The armed forces of Park Rangers are not enough to protect the ivory prongs from these giants of nature. A hundred years ago, the Great White Hunters were the predators. Now the region calls on one man to protect the elephants from virtual extinction ... Tusk.

Note from Author

Generally thought of as the most dangerous animal in the African Big Five, the adult elephant has no natural predators, other than mankind. A protecting mother, territorial male or injured elephant can stomp someone into the ground or toss a human body over the treetops like a child's toy. The majestic beauty of these giants of nature cannot be denied when witnessed in their native habitat from afar.

Hunting has been a valued and often necessary tradition since the beginnings of civilization. There is an unwritten code of ethics and responsibility hunters have to the natural world and a respect for those animals who participate in the dangerous dance of predator and prey. Illegal game poachers have no such reverence for victims harvested mercilessly and sometimes worse; wounded to be left as a dangerous hazard for others.

Akin to my Western stories, *Africa Tusk* is an adventure tale that puts honorable, self-reliant characters into challenged circumstances. While the term hero is a matter of perspective, a moral code of conduct is the measure of a man. The difficult balance of conservation today is life on the verge of radical technology.

Eric H. Heisner   July 21, 2017

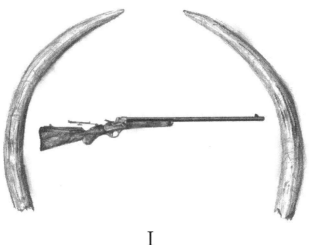

I

The whining grind of shifting gears and the rattle of old metal panels on a vintage Willys Jeep echo into the emptiness. In the midday sun, at a far distance, the all-terrain vehicle bounces through tall grass and crashes through the obstructing brush. The lone figure driving, approaches and tears across the open savannah. Grazing animals scatter in herds as the jeep bounds along, leaving a hot trail of dust in the rising wake.

A broad brim felt hat shadows the features of the man behind the wheel. He looks down at a GPS trans-ponder in hand and steers the narrow axle vehicle up a rocky path to higher ground. Jamming the shifter down a gear, the engine revs as the vehicle climbs upward.

The unrestrained upper torso of the man sways in the seat as the knobbed tires bounce and bump over ragged stones that would tear any normal tire to shreds.

A leather safari boot quickly moves from the gas pedal and jabs onto the foot-break. The locked up tires skid the careening vehicle to a halt just before encountering a jagged mound of large rocks blocking the trail.

A hand passes over the single key in the panel and the motor rattles into silence with exception to the hot ticking wheeze of engine parts. The man leaps from the vehicle and loops his right arm through the dangling strap on a pair of oversized binoculars and grabs up a big bore hunting rifle. With the GPS unit gripped in his other hand and a belt of large caliber ammo slung over his forearm, the man dashes past the pointed rocks and disappears into the brush covered landscape.

An outcropping of sheer faced stone looms over a sheltered valley in east-central Africa. Under the shade of thorny acacia trees, perched between uneven boulder formations, the man peers through the long distance glasses and breathes in short shallow breathes. He tips his broad-brimmed fedora back on his forehead and removes the eyepieces of the viewing glasses from his features. Everett 'Tusk' Kalispell lays out the belt of finger-size cartridges and reaches over to his well-used, late eighteen hundred model, Remington Rolling Block rifle. He flips up the rear tang sight and heaves the long range weapon to his shoulder while squinting along the octagonal barrel at the objects in the far distance below.

Raised in the middle-west of the continental United States, Everett Kalispell learned to stalk game and hunt with the guidance of his grandfather at a young impressionable age. Stories from the olden days, of life on the frontier fueled his imagination and gave the young man a passionate longing for times long past. His skills as a gifted marksman were nurtured along with import-ant teachings on respect for all living creatures.

After years of postgraduate work in ecology and wandering exploration of the American West, he found himself professionally hunting around South America. His reputed skill with a long gun took him to Africa where he became a white hunter whom the locals soon called on as *Tusk*. Of a sturdy mind and stature, suited to the varied and unforgiving continent, the expatriate outdoorsman set up a successful hunting service in a changing land of photo safaris and media heightened green politics. His American drawl and tough stoicism, pro-ducts of his rural upbringing, seemed to serve him well in the remote wilds of Africa.

A figure clad almost entirely in khaki garb book-ended by tall leather safari boots and a fur-felt Stetson. Tusk exhibits his national origin with his choice of head-gear and the wardrobe style of British adventurers from a century past. The afternoon humidity hangs heavy on his sweat-streaked shirt as he stares down at the move-ment in the valley below.

He removes his thorn-scratched head covering to again sight down the length of the long barreled Remington. Beads of sweat form up and trickle down the three day unshaven beard stubble on his cheek. From below, the gut-wrenching sound of a chain-saw starting up and roaring causes him to wince and give a slight shudder of contempt.

Following the gun-sights down to the spread of valley bottom, several bushveld camo-clad poachers gather at the site of a recently massacred rhinoceros family. The black-skinned man wielding a chain-saw bends into his ghastly work of buzzing the forehead of the largest rhino to separate it from the prized horn. Another poacher draws a shiny blade from his hip sheath and cuts meat from the loin of a rhino calf. Laughing and carefree, the remainder of the poacher crew stands near the gathered trucks passing a bottle of homebrewed liquor in celebration.

Finger wrapped on the trigger, Tusk puts the poacher with the chain-saw in his rifle sights and firmly actuates the hammer drop. With a roaring puff of smoke the soft-nosed .45-70 projectile thunders down through the valley and smashes into the unsuspecting target. The gas-powered saw chugs to a halt as the offender flips back and tumbles with half of his chest cavity torn away.

The valley bottom stands eerily silent a moment as the alerted pilferers peer up to the rocky crags above and spot the wispy puff of spent powder smoke rising from the brush. The delayed sound of a rifle shot echoes again as another poacher crashes back against the front fender of the lead truck. There is a flurry of activity as each man bolts to protect themselves by grabbing at military surplus AK-47 auto rifles. The illegal hunters flee to the support vehicles and gunshots erupt in a panicked assembly of defense.

Another hint of smoke drifts skyward from the high rocky bluff and the man behind the wheel of a smuggling truck crashes forward as the exiting bullet buries itself into the metal dashboard. Machine guns aimed skyward, the poachers send long bursts of gunfire up toward the faraway rocks to little effect. The automatic weapons of the horn thieves are systematically quieted by the lethal precision of the long-barreled Rolling Block hunting rifle.

The valley of recent death, now devoid of all gunfire, sits quietly muted as Tusk looks down on the five poachers fatally strewn about the landscape below. He opens the smoking breach of the long range rifle and ejects the empty, burnt-powder tinged casing before he grudgingly slips another long brass cartridge into the hot receiver. With his jaw set hard, Tusk stares silently as he carefully scans the gory carnage of deceased men and slaughtered beast. One of the unlawful hunters, having a bloody wound through a shattered hip, slowly begins to drag himself along the trampled, dry grassy terrain.

A cooling breeze passes over the high rock perch and Tusk raises his eye momentarily from the lineup of the gun's sights. He looks down at the ruthlessly slain grouping of rhinoceros and grimaces with contempt. With no more hesitation than the extermination of a disease infested rodent, Tusk places the last surviving poacher in his rifle sights and pulls the trigger.

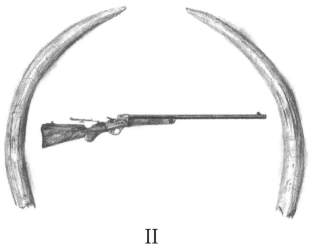

II

A compound of mud-brick buildings assembled like a Spanish hacienda sits nestled in an oasis of shading, flat-top trees on the edge of the savannah. Several battered guide service trucks sit parked under pole-beam shelters and a barracks type structure stretches long and narrow behind the low roofed barn. On a slightly raised berm of ground, perched atop a solid stone foundation, sits an adobe constructed ranch house with a wide shaded porch contiguous on all sides. The earthen, sunbaked tile roof is supported by wooden timbers that extend well beyond the hand-hewn planked decking below.

In front of the ranch house sits the topless jeep and the clank of vehicle maintenance can be heard under an oddly canted truck at a nearby pole barn shelter. Slanted rays of daylight from the late afternoon sun angle on the horizon as two, dark-tinted Land Rovers drive along the dry, dirt lane leading toward the safari station. A shrill whistling call of alert sounds a warning and resonances across the quiet homestead. At the doors of the barracks, several dark, native domestics appear from the shadows and watch with bright curious eyes.

Tusk steps out from the dim interior of the main house to the shaded porch and watches the long steady approach of the uninvited visitors. He holds a cocktail glass floating a lone cube of ice in one hand and a M1911 auto pistol dropped at his side in the other. He stands alone on the deck waiting, calm and quiet, studying the black window tinted government-issue vehicles.

The clinking sound of the cut ice on the thick-walled cocktail glass resonates in the porch shadows as Tusk swirls his drink before raising it to his lips. A heavy powder of gravel dust covers the dark windows as the pair of Land Rovers rolls up in front of the main house and idles to a stop. The trailing road haze settles before opposing doors open to reveal two government men in suits and reflective sunglasses. The two dark-skinned agents move forward and stand like obedient statues near the front panel of the vehicles. Their trim cut suits do nothing to hide the telling bulge of a firearm tucked away in a shoulder holster.

A uniformed official steps out of the rear drivers side of the closest vehicle and lets his door swing closed behind him. The auto pistol is still held non-threatening at Tusk's side as he takes another long sip of his amber cocktail. He stares down at the officer and gazes at the passenger side door as another elusive figure steps out but remains concealed behind the darkened window glass of the vehicle.

The officially uniformed government agent, Jimmy Franks, steps forward with a wide toothy grin and waves a friendly greeting up toward the lone figure standing on the expansive porch.

"Haloo there … Tusk, my friend. Glad to find you around the home place."

Jimmy Franks steps away from the vehicle and past the stationary government sentinel. He keeps smiling as he continues to talk through his big gleaming choppers.

"My apologies for not radioing first, but it seems when we announce our visits beforehand you are out and about in the bush for days, sometimes weeks."

A slight grin comes over Tusk's features as he takes another swallow from his glass tumbler.

"Jimmy Franks … you and your entourage are always welcome for a *short* visit."

The government official noticeably relaxes with Tusk's casual tone of reception and coolly gestures the two posted men at ease.

"Ahh, good to see I caught you in a good humor. Sometimes I don't always feel welcome."

"Sometimes, you're not ..."

From his vantage on the elevated porch, Tusk eyes the rear passenger side door and observes the figure behind shift to a feminine stance. A quizzical look crosses his features and he glances back toward Jimmy Franks.

"Who did you bring along with you?"

The government official wipes a trickle of sweat away from under his chin and widens his already enormous grin. Jimmy Franks takes another step forward and maneuvers a sort of bowing salute back toward the open passenger side door on the vehicle.

"I present to you this fine day, Doctor Roosevelt Hamilton Adams."
The dust covered Land Rover door swings back to reveal the unforeseen individual and Tusk nearly drops his cradled beverage in bewildered shock.

Presented before him, Doctor Adams is a simply beautiful woman whose fair skin stands in stark contrast to the dark complected men she accompanies. Her tall female figure is dressed in colonial safari garb which is tucked and put together so all the hills and valleys are geographically perfect. Her length of light colored hair is pulled behind and swirled under an English styled pith sun helmet.

The vehicle door bangs shut and Tusk is jolted from his fanciful gaze. The doctor steps around to the front of the vehicle and moves with a hip swaggering stride. She pauses alongside Jimmy Franks and he extends his arm to escort her toward the adobe constructed house. At the bottom of the wide set of stairs that ascend to the veranda, they stop and she glimpses around with a keen perceptiveness while smiling up at their host.

"It is a most anticipated pleasure and a sincere honor to meet you, Mister Kalispell."

Tusk studies her curiously and sets his drink aside on the wide wooden porch rail. Standing before the guests, he self-consciously looks down at his sidearm before awkwardly tucking the pistol into his pants waistband. He smoothes his loosely draped shirt tails around the gun and partially conceals it.

She eyes the firearm with interest and winks with a sparkle of mischievousness.

"Expecting trouble?"

Tusk catches her eye and jauntily tilts his head in return.

"Always."

Her smile wanes, then renews as she peers up at him.

"Do you often greet visitors in this manner?"

"I wasn't expecting anyone."

"Is this a bad time?"

"That depends ... what are you a doctor of?"

Jimmy Franks continues to grin amused at the flirtatious tone of the probing banter and laughs.

"Mister Kalispell doesn't get many female callers here in the remotest of locations."

The government officer turns to his agents and dismisses them with a wave. Tusk frowns toward Jimmy's insinuation and cast a friendly gaze toward the doctor.

"Not many uninvited."

A cool afternoon breeze washes through the shaded veranda and Doctor Adams peers up at Tusk with a seductive sort of glimmer.

"My deepest apologies for not being proper and announcing ourselves first, Mister Kalispell."

Heaving a cordial sigh, Tusk inadvertently gawks at the attractive-looking lady doctor and can't help but offer a welcoming smile.

"Drop the Mister Kalispell stuff and call me *Tusk*. Please excuse my coarse manner, but it's been a tough week. You've most likely had a long trip from some-where … come inside and have a drink."

His eyes travel toward the government official beside her and he unconsciously grimaces.

"I guess you can come in too, Franks."

Jimmy Franks grins and bows low as he watches the attractive female visitor climb the steps before him.

"I thought you'd never ask."

In the overhanging shade, Tusk steps aside as the pair ascend the stairs to the wide boards of the entryway. He ushers the doctor inside through the open French doors and reaches his hand out to Jimmy's uniform sleeve to stop him short.

"You going to tell me what this is about?"

The government official continues his broad grin as he talks through his pearly white teeth.

"I am strictly Ambassador on this one. They are still doing mountains of paperwork on that other recent business of yours."

They each eye the enigmatic female guest waiting patiently inside. Tusk nods acquiescent and Jimmy Franks walks confidently into the house as if entering familiar home surroundings. Still in the shade of the veranda, Tusk pauses a moment, grabs his cocktail glass from the porch railing and follows them both inside.

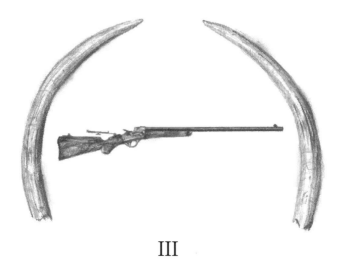

III

The swirl of tawny spirits fills stout tumblers to healthy pours as the neck of the decanter clanks to each lip of glass. The heavy drinking vessels sit lined in a row on a carved mahogany sideboard as their host finishes the bartending chore. Tusk scoops up two of the cocktails and serves the drinks to the government official and his attractive guest. He tops off his own glass and walks over to a large padded leather chair.

Tusk takes a sip from his refilled beverage and pulls the slab-sided auto pistol from the waist of his khaki trousers. Nonchalantly, he places the firearm on the side table and settles into the creaking leather seat. He glances at Jimmy Franks who continues his ceaseless grin, then looks over to the lady doctor.

"So ... you're a doctor, Doctor Adams?"

"Mister Tusk, you can just call me Roosevelt."

"No Mister required here."

Roosevelt casts her eyes around the room at the various exotic animal skins and trophy mounts on the wall.

"I don't really answer to Doctor either."

"Roosevelt then … hmm? That's almost longer than just saying Doctor Adams."

"It's a close second."

Tusk ponders her accent and watches as she paces the great room studying its contents of game trophies and native artwork. The banter is deferred as he takes another healthy sip from his afternoon cocktail.

"You're not South African … English?"

"Yes, Durham."

"Looking to recolonize down here?"

Roosevelt gracefully turns her gaze upon Tusk as he settles back contentedly in the leather chair. She takes a swallow from her own cocktail glass and assesses the brand of character before her.

The doctor holds her drink mid chest and stares across the room at the safari game host.

"I'm a Specialist … here in Africa to do research on some of the exotic diseases affecting the animals."

Tusk looks skeptically over at Jimmy Franks who has moved closer to lean on the sideboard.

"You brought me an animal doctor?"

The thud of the glass tumbler on the bar-top is followed by an innocent shrug from the uniformed agent.

"I've brought you less interesting subjects."

Roosevelt watches their tense exchange of expressions and swirls the iced contents of the glass in hand. She flushes slightly at the condescending tone detected between the two men and clears her throat.

"A Doctor of sorts ..."

The leather chair creaks as Tusk throws one leg over the other, flexes the ankle of his tall safari boot and settles in more comfortable. He takes a sip, rubs the fresh stubble on his chin and stares across at Roosevelt.

"I haven't seen any strange wildlife sicknesses. The only thing ailing … or should I say, any serious threats to the animal populations in Africa are strictly man-made."

Jimmy Franks lifts his glass to take a drink and sets his tumbler back on the wooden sideboard again. He smoothes his manicured hand down the front of his crisp uniform and sends a wizened look toward Tusk, then addresses Roosevelt.

"Yes, and as your host here well knows, it is a disease sometimes cured by a good dose of lead from a far distance."

Tusk balances his cocktail glass on his knee and peers through the wavy glass at the government official.

"There haven't been any relapses in those cases."

"Effective, but not strictly legal."

The professional hunter raises his line of sight and narrows his eyes toward Jimmy Franks.

"Justified by the Laws of Nature."

"But not those Laws of Man."

Roosevelt makes a polite sniff and sets her drink aside on one of the low side tables.

"I don't mean to interrupt your debate on morality, but I wanted to talk about elephants."

Africa Tusk

The mention of the large animal gets Tusk's attention and he turns to her, raising an eyebrow.

"Morality and the eminent fate of elephants are one in the same."

Roosevelt stares at the two opposites of men in the room and continues with an explanation of her assignment.

"Survival of these majestic animals is my focus."

Jimmy Franks leans down on the carved sideboard and smiles while Tusk takes another swallow from his drink and squints curiously at the doctor.

"What about them in particular?"

The tall, slender woman gracefully saunters around the sofa and eases herself onto the couch, seated catty-corner from the storied hunter.

"There is a steady decline in their population."

Tusk sits up a bit and cradles his beverage on his lap.

"Their decimation hasn't been from any sort of exotic disease. Over fifty thousand elephants were killed last year by illegal poaching."

A rising ferocity starts to hint in Tusk's voice.

"That is an outrageously unbelievable number that has continued for decades. I grew up in a town in the States with a tenth less population than that."

The room takes on an uneasy stillness when Tusk leans forward and stares into Roosevelt's attentive eyes. His heartfelt passion for his adopted home in Africa and the native wildlife burns fervently in his demeanor. Roosevelt sits firmly, unflinching under his penetrating gaze as Tusk continues.

"Can you imagine the poachers taking down these gorgeous creatures with smuggled, military-grade machine guns? They just devastate them, slaughtering whole herds. They kill the bulls, then the mamas with calves 'nd all … just for the ivory."

Tusk glances over to Jimmy Franks at the stocked sideboard who nods gravely. He turns back toward Roosevelt, eases back into the leather chair with a creak and takes a calming breath to regain his composure.

"Do you know where most of the ivory goes? I'll tell you where the exotic disease is."

Extending an arm over to a tabletop globe, Tusk gives it a spin and jabs his finger on the Asian continent.

"They sell it in China to make chopsticks and tourist trinkets. Imagine, sacrificing these beautiful animals to make inconsequential garbage."

Roosevelt locks eyes with Tusk and nods sadly.

"I understand and would like to help."

Not being able to stifle a contemptuous laugh, Tusk raises his drink and takes a long swallow.

"And how is that, Doctor?"

Roosevelt looks intently at her host.

"Along with treating any disease, we have an experimental procedure and drug that may hamper the growth of the animal's ivory."

Through a squinted gaze, Tusk studies the seriousness of her good intentions.

"Stunt tusk growth, huh?"

"No tusks, no ivory trade."

"There already happen to be some in the herd without tusks but they aren't the ones that are best suited for the three 'F's."

"What are those?"

"Forage, fight and ... well, you know the other."

Jimmy Franks raises his glass with a wide beaming grin and salutes his host.

"Well said and always classy."

Tusk shoots a gaze over at the government agent and turns his attentions back to Roosevelt, looking skeptical.

"How have these experimental drugs been tested? I haven't seen too many lab rats comparable in mass to an elephant."

"Texas feral hogs."

The professional hunter fiddles with the glass tumbler in his lap and glances back at Jimmy Franks who merely shrugs and continues to smile.

"Any side effects on their other teeth?"

"Only on the protruding ones."

A hint of a drunken smile crosses the hunter's features.

"There's more'n a few folks in Alabama who may need your services. Why don't you test it on them first?"

The English doctor tilts her head quizzically and seems to miss the backwoods reference. She looks over at her host with a calming seriousness to her gaze.

"We're not exactly sure of the effect on elephants in the wild as only a few animals have been tested in zoos. It may even alter the offspring so they don't grow them either but we haven't had success yet with reproducing the traits in captivity."

A slight draft passes through the open pair of doors as Tusk mentally processes what he's hearing. He sips from his cocktail glass and eases back in the leather chair before turning to address Roosevelt.

"So, you and your team of doctors and scientists are planning to change centuries of biological makeup in these giants among men?"

"We call it an evolutionary drift, and for this job in particular it's just me."

"And you think you're up for the task?"

The gentle evening breeze fades away and the stifling remainder of heat in the great room hangs heavy as Roosevelt faces off with Tusk.

"If we don't do something about it soon, they will be killed to extinction and then there is no drug that can bring them back alive."

Thoughts of interfering with nature weigh heavy on Tusk's mind as he looks away and sits deep in the chair. In one grand swallow, he finishes his drink and sets the empty glass on the side table next to his handgun.

"Hell, I'm game for a story. Tell me your plan."

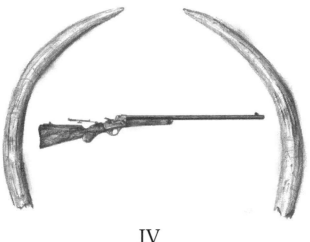

IV

The sunlight outside fades to evening as oil lamps in the house are lit by a young domestic houseboy. Tusk and Roosevelt stand across from the uniformed government official at the dining room table where they study a detailed map of east-central Africa. Tusk leans one hand down on the rough-hewn plank slab and reaches out his other over the geographic chart. He taps his finger on the coastline and looks up at the pair listening.

"Most of the ivory is smuggled out at Mombasa through shipping containers. Once it makes it to port, it is pretty much on a free ride to the Chinese market."

The professional hunter glances up at Jimmy Franks who doesn't respond with his trademark smile at the accusatorial implication. The government official let's his eyes connect with Tusk then drop back to the map as their host continues.

"Either seized or sold, it doesn't matter to the dead elephants. We're way over here and can't really influence what happens on the coast."

The doctor leans down and studies the map details.

"Where are the elephant herds most at risk?"

Tusk gestures his hand over a wide swath of territory further inland past Tsavo National Park and Mt. Meru.

"There are Government Ranger patrols all around but they are out-gunned and don't have the funding or manpower to protect all the herds as they are constantly moving. Most of the poachers work on the fringes of Kenya, Tanzania and Mozambique where the higher-ups are powerless against the wealth, smuggled ivory can bring, and lowly officials are an easy bribe."

The visiting government agent coughs, stands uncomfortable and raises a warning eyebrow toward Tusk. The hunter suppresses a smirk, places both hands on the table and flexes his back. He stares across the map at Jimmy Franks then turns his head to Roosevelt.

"Of course that sort of thing doesn't happen around here that often."

Jimmy Franks stands erect on the opposite side of the table, with his hands grasped behind his back.

"We do our best to protect the environment and be good stewards of Africa and her wildlife resources."

"Sometimes your best ain't getting the job done."

"If you are implying that we encourage vulgar tactics implemented by vigilante game hunters, you are treading on dangerous territory."

Africa Tusk

The tension between the two men steadily boils until Roosevelt comes around the end of the table and pats Jimmy Franks tenderly on the arm.

"We are all here to figure out a way to protect these magnificent animals the best way we can."

Tusk ignores her obvious diplomacy and points to a large unpopulated area on the inland portion of the map. He raps his extended finger on the table for emphasis and looks up at the others with a serious glare.

"If you want to protect the most endangered herds, you need to focus your attention here. Hundreds of Rangers have been killed around this area doing their job in the last decade. It is a war-zone of illegal poaching and you'd better be ready to defend yourself."

The room is silent a long moment as the glowing flicker from the oil lamps takes over for the darkening skies outside. Roosevelt turns to Tusk and unveils a seductive air accompanied by a sympathetic smile.

"I don't plan to go in there alone. That's why I need you Mister Kalispell … uh, I'm sorry, *Tusk*."

"Need me for what?"

She taps a slender digit on the map in the area Tusk had referred and peers up at the revered white hunter.

"I would like to hire you to take me to that region so I can survey the endangered elephant populations."

The conflicted safari hunter rubs his hand across his mouth and lets his short fingernails rake down the whisker growth on his cheek.

Tusk stands before Roosevelt, looks down at the map and frowns over at Jimmy Franks, skeptically.

"You … and what army?"

The lady doctor shakes her head confident, turns her attention to Jimmy Franks then back at Tusk.

"No military involvement whatsoever ... just me and the supplies needed to do my work."
Jimmy Franks can't refrain his beaming smile and Tusk appears genuinely stunned. He stares across the table speechless and almost stammers when he finally addresses the lady doctor.

"Ma'am, I don't think you fully understand ... Nobody goes there unless they have to and I wouldn't take anyone to that region without ample preparations."

"Why is that?"

"It's very dangerous."

"You mean, because I'm a woman?"

Tusk looks to Jimmy Franks for his support but only receives that stupid grin in return. The professional hunter blatantly nods toward Roosevelt.

"You *are* a woman."

"I know that, Mister Kalispell."
A gentle wind rattles the glass panels on the closed double doors and Tusk gathers his thoughts.

"What I mean and you don't seem to understand, is that it's not safe for anyone who can't handle firearms adequately if we get into a tight spot."

The chatter of nocturnal insects and wildlife outside begins to fill the night air as Roosevelt glares silently at Tusk. She calmly walks away from the long wooden slab of a dining table and picks up Tusk's M1911 .45 automatic handgun from next to his chair in the adjacent room. She jacks the slide on the receiver back, slamming a loaded cartridge into the chamber and points the barrel up at an exotic prong-horned shoulder mount on the far, great room wall.

Tusk takes a measured step toward her in an attempt to calm the situation and take the firearm away.

"Alright, alright … you can cock a gun."

She sends a sidelong glance at Tusk then squeezes off a deafening shot which blasts the tip off the right horn. Tusk stops short, shocked at her aim and audacity.

Off-hand, Roosevelt resumes her target, fires the handgun again and continuously chips away at the length of the right horn. She starts in on the left and empties the ammunition clip. A cloud of spent gunpowder fills the air and Tusk grits his teeth as he stares up at the irreparable damage to his prized mount.

Ears still ringing, Tusk takes the hot-barreled firearm from her hand and walks to a bureau near the wall and opens one of the compartments. He slides out the empty magazine from the pistol's handle, tosses it inside the drawer and inserts a fully loaded ammo clip. Turning to the room, he shakes his head as he gapes at the inimitable brash woman.

"I'll be sure to make a visit your home sometime and shoot up any priceless art you may have hanging on your walls."

Roosevelt remains poised in the haze of gun-smoke and stands rigid as she responds.

"I will pay for the damages to your art as well as the wall. I believe in being direct."

With an annoyed huff, Tusk pushes the handgun into his belted waistband and waves his arm toward the window at the rear of the house.

"I have a shooting range for that sort of thing the next time you want to be direct."

"Will you take me to the elephants?"

Tusk looks over at Jimmy Franks who stares up at the defiled wall trophy with a dumb grin. The safari hunter turns his attention to Roosevelt and shakes his head.

"Not without a crew, I won't."

Roosevelt nods empathetically and smoothes her hands down the button front of her khaki shirt jacket.

"I will pay for whatever support crew you deem necessary. Complete compensation will be handled by my organization."

There is a heavy pounding on the planked stairs outside and a shuffling scrape of feet across the front porch. Everyone turns as the set of French doors burst open from the exterior. A gruff bearded man clad in unkempt undergarments stumbles in as the double doors rattle back on the hinges. With a Winchester pump trench gun in hand, the confused intruder looks around wide-eyed still seemingly half-asleep.

An experienced tracker of game and African sportsman, Butch McGuinn has lived around the sparsely populated backcountry of the Dark Continent the greater portion of his many years. He quickly zeros in on the feminine form of Doctor Adams at the center of the room and raises an inquisitive eyebrow toward Tusk.

"Didn't know you was hostin' a soiree with a lady. What's all the shooting about?"

Tusk adjusts the gun in his waistband and tilts his head toward the single pronged game mount, up on the wall.

"Our lady guest here was making a statement."

Africa Tusk

The half-dressed man seems to still be in the process of waking up and stares around with confusion. Tusk gestures his hand toward a shattered pile of horn on the floor and up at the one horned game trophy backed by fresh bullet holes in the wall. Lowering the pump shotgun, Butch steps further into the room and looks up with a saddened expression.

"Aww, tis a shame. T'was a beautiful rack."

Butch turns and glances over at Roosevelt and impulsively looks to her ample chest before moving his attentions up to her face.

"Hmm, a nice rack indeed … Who are you?"

The scattergun wielding game hunter suddenly notices Jimmy Franks watching from across the room with the ever-present, but silent smile. His amorous gaze turns to animosity as he turns his attentions to the officer.

"I saw yer damned trucks outside ya grinnin' son of a bitch. Hoped I'd be able to get a shot or two off in yer direction at least."

Jimmy Franks beams wider and offers a waving salute.

"Not today unfortunately … Sorry."

Roosevelt approaches Butch, lets her studied gaze drop to his tee-shirt and stained undergarments then extends an outstretched hand.

"You may call me Roosevelt, and whom do I have the pleasure of meeting in finest evening attire?"

Putting out his large paw of a hand, Butch gawks down at her womanly figure posed in striking safari garb.

"Me name's Butch McGuinn, my friends call me Butchie, but you can call me Sir."

She raises an eyebrow, mirroring his comical gaze.

"If you keep staring at my chest like you are, then I'll just call you Butch."

"Fair enough."

The gray haze of smoke has mostly cleared from the air and Tusk moves across the room to sit in his padded leather armchair. Removing the handgun from his waist, he places his gun across his knee. The brief exchange of introductions has ceased and he cranes his neck to address the underwear clad man in the doorway.

"Butch, close the door, she's our new employer."

"Really? For what?"

"We're gonna go hunt for elephants."

The broad shouldered man looks bewildered as he continues to grip Roosevelt's slender hand firmly in his big mitt. As if still in a dreamy daze, Butch watches Tusk twirl the automatic pistol and set it on the side table while Jimmy Franks walks over and sits on the sofa. He crinkles his brow as he stares at the cordial government agent.

"He ain't here to issue no papers or fines?"

Jimmy Franks smooths his shirt front and smiles.

"Purely a social call."

Tusk turns his composed regard from Butch to the government agent with his unfaltering grin.

"I guess you'll all want to spend the night?"

Jimmy Franks licks his wide spreading lips and tries to tame gleaming choppers that he can't seem to restrain.

"What's for breakfast?"

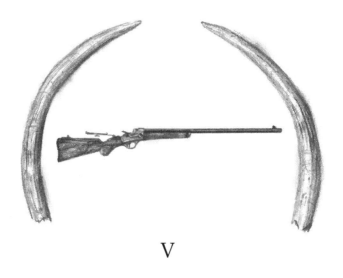

V

The black government vehicles sit parked behind the main house near the outbuildings where the safari guide trucks are formed up for loading. Tusk walks over to the rear of the black Land Rover as Roosevelt continues to supervise the unpacking of waterproof Pelican cases. He stops and stares amazed at the growing stockpile of mysterious gear boxes containing tech support.

One of Tusk's safari crew approaches and grabs another armful of Roosevelt's items. The professional hunter watches the cases being loaded into the supply truck parked behind his Willys Jeep and looks over the mounting pile quizzically.

"What is all this stuff?"

Roosevelt leans back on the bumper of the truck.

"My gear needed for the job."

"You're going to set up a computer lab?"

"Tracking and analyzing the proper data is very technical work. I'll need more than a calculator."

Tusk chews his lip as he mentally assesses the cargo space needed to travel with all her extra support items.

"Can't you leave some of this here at the ranch?"

The doctor takes a moment to scan her eyes over the multitude of computer cases and watertight boxes. She stands and reaches into the back of the Land Rover to pull out two rifle cases, then adds them to the pile.

"No."

Tusk shakes his head as he studies the nondescript containers of gear. He eyes several canisters looking to be ammunition and turns to Roosevelt questioningly.

"What's with the gun cases and the ammo boxes? I'm bringing plenty of those sorts of things along."

Roosevelt stops marking on her checklist and turns to Tusk in his irritated state.

"These are special tranquilizer rifles and the mixed doses are in those ammo cases."

"Planning to knockout every elephant in Africa?"

"Every single one I can get in sight range of."

"Well, when we're done here, I'll drive you over to India to use the rest of it.

She rolls her eyes and resumes her task of unloading.

"These are the tools for the job and materials I need unless *you* want to sneak up on them personally and give the injections by hand."

Another ranch worker approaches to load his arms with gear and Roosevelt directs him which cases to bring next. The man speaks in a reluctant tone and Roosevelt answers him in a surprisingly fluent Swahili.

Africa Tusk

Tusk listens interested as the hired hand expresses there isn't enough room in the vehicles for everything. Roosevelt turns from the noncompliant ranch worker to Tusk.

"Do I need to invite Mister Franks and the military along for their support? They seem more than interested in supervising your activities."
Tusk heaves a sigh and looks to the last remaining truck in the pole barn, up on jacks for maintenance work.

"I'll have 'em bring along the other truck."
In a bit of a huff, Tusk walks away to talk with his crew leaving Roosevelt to finish supervising the transfer of her supplies from the government utility vehicles.

Well into midday, the last of the gear and equipment is loaded onto the trucks and each vehicle sits parked along the lineup with the driver and safari crew mulling around in the created shade nearby. Tusk walks over with a tall, dark-skinned crewmember to where Roosevelt inspects the cargo inside one of the trucks.

"Doctor Roosevelt Hamilton Adams, this is Mogambo. He is my friend and gun bearer who will be your personal protector when I am not around and will watch over your supplies."

"Please, just call me Roosevelt."
The doctor extends her hand to Mogambo and he grips it most enthusiastically. Roosevelt studies the welcoming native crewman and smiles.

"I'm pleased to work with you, Mogambo. It sounds familiar, where did you get such a name?"

A sly grin crosses Tusk's features and he puts his hand on Mogambo's broad, slender shoulder.

"His real name is Clark Gable."

Roosevelt looks to Mogambo questioningly.

"Really?"

"Yes, Memsahib."

"You're kidding me?"

Mogambo smiles kindly.

"No, Memsahib."

She watches Tusk a moment and then turns back to her personal escort with a curious tone.

"Do you speak much English?"

"Yes, Memsahib."

Tusk takes his hand from Mogambo's shoulder and steps around to examine the abundance of scientific materials in the back of the safari vehicle.

"Understands fine. Not much of a chit-chatter."

He inspects the bed of the packed cargo hold and gives the raised tailgate a rap with his knuckles.

"Well, if you're all loaded and ready, Mogambo will drive this truck and you can ride up in the Jeep."

"With you?"

With a haughty stance, Roosevelt looks to the Jeep and the convoy of vehicles strung along behind.

"I may prefer to ride back here with Mogambo."

The dark-skinned escort steps to the driver's door and opens it with a loud creak. He tosses his shoulder bag across the passenger seat and looks back to Roosevelt.

"No, Memsahib."

Tusk looks to the doctor and gives a slight chuckle.

"Well, there you go ... he has spoken."

Africa Tusk

The white hunter flips a salute to Mogambo then turns away and walks toward the front of the convoy. He pauses at each truck and gives orders to the guide hands along the way. Like a wagon train from the days of American westward expansion, the group forms up behind the wagon-master, ready to pull out.

The expedition of safari vehicles bounces along the vast grassy landscapes shrouded in a cloud of dry dust that rises up from rattling axles and turning wheels. Tusk steers the topless Willys Jeep at the lead, followed by Butch driving the truck with support gear. Behind them, another truck holds several members of the safari crew and Mogambo brings up the rear with the extra load of doctor supplies. Herds of grazing wildlife scatter in every direction as the cavalcade travels deeper into the feral territory of Africa.

The Willys Jeep drives nimbly through the road-less landscape as Tusk maneuvers around rocks, termite mounds and sinkholes in the navigated path. On the dashboard, a compass orb bobbles constantly from the irregular route. Roosevelt watches as Tusk deftly steers around another road obstacle a fleeting moment before impact. She grips the side of the windshield as the jeep continues to bounce along.

"Have you been out to this area much?"

Tusk keeps his eyes on their course and raises his voice above the rattle of undercarriage and engine noise.

"No ... a few times. They call it the 'Poacher's Playpen'. If I wanted that kind of action, there is plenty of it near enough to me at the ranch."

"Cute name for it."

"Yeah, I guess not to scare the tourists."

Roosevelt's upper torso bobbles around in the passenger seat and she catches Tusk hide an amused grin while driving across the uneven terrain. The narrow framed vehicle continues to travel along with a swirl of dust all around. She wipes the bandana around her neck across her eyes and dabs her mouth.

"What kind of place is it?"

"It's all Africa … simply beautiful."

"Except?"

Tusk glances over at her and shrugs.

"It's a good place to get killed and the wildlife is only part of the dangers there. A land filled with lions, leopards and mercenaries. Kinda like the Wild West except with automatic rifles and pirates. "

"Can't the local governments clamp down on the gun trade and illegal poaching activity?"

The jeep engine roars as Tusk downshifts to gain momentum over an incline. He stares ahead as he talks.

"The local governments do the best they can until someone pays them a lot of money to do different."

He squeezes his palms and flexes his knuckles to the thin steering wheel, obviously irritated by the thought of the rampant poaching situation.

"I've seen government agents chase away, gun down and arrest poachers then turn around and sell the confiscated ivory right out of their own trucks. There is a huge market in countries far away from here that have no care about the African situation or local economy."

Africa Tusk

Tusk shakes his head perturbed and wipes the tails from his own neckerchief across the lens of his eye goggles.

"The ridiculous amounts of blood money are basically raping Africa of its resources and integrity."

The doctor pivots in her seat to look behind at the safari vehicles bounding along in the followed path.

"What do you think should be done to stop it?" Tusk jiggles the loose steering wheel over rutted terrain, pauses to think then gives her a sidelong glance.

"If you really want to stop the killing, you have to convince a billion Chinamen that bamboo chopsticks taste better than ivory."

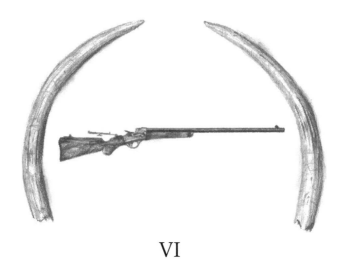

VI

The convoy of safari vehicles travels across shallow rivulets and picturesque landscapes of the African continent as the fading light of day turns to evening. Multitudes of grazing wildlife coexist on the wide grassy savannah, creating a breathtaking and exotic site to the foreign eye. The vintage Jeep and safari trucks steer toward a cluster of broad shading trees ahead with low rolling mountains on the horizon in the far, far distance.

Grinding the gear-shifter down to a lower gear, Tusk eases the jeep to a rolling stop near one of the large overhanging trees. He rises behind the wheel, places one foot on the driver's seat and scans the vacant terrain in all directions. The following trucks idle in their tracks as Tusk studies the unpeopled lands.

"We'll camp here for the night."

Africa Tusk

Satisfied with the location, he raises his right hand from his grip along the top of the windshield and whirls an overhead, circular gesture to the others. The trucks drive alongside and past the jeep to group the safari vehicles in a defensive formation. Butch gives a waving salute as he maneuvers his truck into position and Mogambo offers a slight nod to their leader in the jeep as he parks several meters in front.

The faint glow of twilight is still upon the safari camp as the white canvas tents are finally assembled and support ropes are lashed taut. A small intimate fire near the center of the site sends illuminating light just out past the circle of vehicles. Mogambo tends to setup preparations while the three other native crewmen work quietly with sparse spoken words.

Roosevelt sits in a cloth slung camp chair with her hat on her knee and a tin cup in hand near the fire circle. Just to her right, Butch works on a portable stove-top attached to a fold-down prep table at the side of the supply truck. He lights the flame on the propane gas ring and settles a large cast iron skillet over the grate.

Working on a small butcher-board surface attach-ed to the burner setup, he begins chopping and peeling ingredients. He wipes his forearm across his sweat drenched forehead and glances past his shoulder at the lady doctor seated in the chair.

"So, how do you like this Africa so far?" Roosevelt smiles and adjusts herself in the canvas seat.

"I've been to Africa on several occasions. This is my first time to this region though."

Butch continues to chop and scrape ingredients into the dark, seasoned pan.

"Well, this is the most beautiful part of it unless you like big jungle gorillas, mosquito-infested rivers, overcrowded cities or old pyramids and sand traps."

She nods amused and sips from her cup as Butch continues his task. The burly man stretches his back and glances out past the light of camp into the darkness, searching for something. He shifts the skillet handle away from the heat and flashes a grin at Roosevelt.

"So … I hear you're a doctor of sorts and think you can save some elephants?"

"I hope to."

"Ain't worried none 'bout messin' with nature … considerin' that you might kill 'em mistakenly with the drugs or make 'em less of what they are meant to be by changin' them like that?"

"I don't see much of a choice."

Butch stabs his knife into the cutting block and swipes the chopped bits into the pan. He shrugs his broad shoulders and looks over at the female doctor.

"There's always a choice to it, but not always good ones. Ya ever think you might be putting a hefty price tag on the ones that still have their ivory."

Roosevelt reflects and takes another sip from her cup as the thought of her actions unintentionally hurting more animals unsettles her. She glances around the camp, seeing only one worker lighting kerosene lamps, and stares into the blackness which is alive with the sounds of nature. She listens into the night wondering where everyone went while cradling the shiny tin mug.

Africa Tusk

"What kind of man is Mister Kalispell?"

Butch laughs as he continues his task of meal prep.

"Tusk? He's a tough son of a bitch for starts."

Roosevelt looks down at the fire and swirls the dark contents in her cup.

"I've heard all types of stories about him in Mombasa. Some are a bit more fanciful than others."

"Well, you can believe about half of 'em. There ain't much unusual news around, so when an American white hunter makes a headline, others are quick to make up tales of their own."

The nocturnal sounds of the wild begin to elevate from the darkness and Roosevelt clears her throat to speak.

"Some call him a murderer ..."

Butch pauses his cooking and his tone becomes grave.

"That's an ugly word now, ain't it?"

He turns down the fire under the cooking pan and pivots to face Roosevelt. She stares up at him and sits fixed in the chair as the big man looms large opposite her.

"You know Ma'am ... humans used to kill for survival and now they find everything they need in grocery stores. Folks conveniently forget that someone had to do the dirty work of getting it to the bar-b-que for whatever special holiday they're celebratin'."

Butch wipes his thick hands on his short leather apron front and lets his eyes search the darkness. The night sounds chatter loudly as the camp seems devoid of all crew occupants. After a short time, he returns his attentions to the woman in the camp chair with the prevailing urban mentality.

"Tusk does what he's good at, but hunting animals is only the part of it. When you've been in the bush a bit longer, you'll see that the circle of life here is a quick and violent loop ... to keep on the circuit you have to be ruthless sometimes."

"I've heard that he's killed men."

Butch watches her silently then finally turns and stirs the sizzling contents of the pan as he notices Tusk approach in the far reaches of light. With liquor bottle in hand, the professional hunter walks to the fire circle and the glint of flames play off his hard masculine features.

Tusk takes a healthy swig from the half-empty bottle and notices his presence causing an awkward pause to the conversation. A slight sway in his stance, he tosses a jesting jab toward his cooking companion.

"Hey there Butchie, what kind of mystery stew do you have to experiment on us tonight?"

The new arrival to the fire circle looks down at Roosevelt then back to Butch and quickly senses the somber mood.

"Did I interrupt something?"

The cast iron pan sizzles as Butch stirs. Looking over his shoulder at Tusk, Butch pulls the knife from the cutting board and directs it toward their female guest.

"The lady here was just questioning your history and relationship with eradicating poachers."

Mid-sip from her cup, Roosevelt nearly chokes as Butch calls out her allegation of manslaughter and puts her directly on the spot. Sitting uneasy in her chair, she coughs and sputters in defense.

"No offense intended, I just, uh ..."

Africa Tusk

Tusk glances toward Butch and seats himself in a camp chair opposite Roosevelt. He pushes back relaxed with a creak of the wood construction and kicks his tall boots out. Feet crossed at the ankles, he stares across the jumping flames at the doctor. His eyes seem glassy as they shimmer in the firelight.

"I've been accused of a lot of things that aren't true ... eliminating a blood for hire poacher is something I'm not afraid to admit is a fact.

Tusk lets his words sink in as Mogambo appears out of the darkness behind. He senses his native friend, glances over to the edge of camp and continues speaking toward Roosevelt.

"There is no game sport in gunning down an animal with military caliber automatic rifles just to hack a market valued item from its dying carcass."

"I didn't mean to accuse you."
The slightly intoxicated hunter takes another pull at the swirling amber contents of the bottle.

"I know of the rumored talk and some of it is partly true. Believe me ... if I have an opportunity to even the odds, I won't hesitate to pull the trigger."

"How do you catch illegal hunters in the act?"

"Many of the herds are tagged with locator chips to monitor their migration patterns and numbers. When their vitals drop from the charts and I'm in a position to do something about it, I get an anonymous tip to what's going on along with the coordinates."

"You get a call from the government?"

Butch pours from another jug into a tin cup and hands it to Tusk. He takes the half empty bottle from his friend and looks down at Roosevelt as he walks past.

"Are you a doctor or a journalist?"

She watches Butch at the cooktop and turns back.

"I'm just interested in saving animals."

Tusk takes a drink and kicks at one of the logs in the fire.

"Let's just say the animals in the parks near the ranch are mostly left alone."

She looks over as the silent form of Mogambo joins the men gathered around another small campfire. The dark-skinned crewmen shimmer in the orange firelight as they eat and speak in muted voices. Sitting on the ground before small pup tents, the native crew has their own social faction.

Butch scoops a bowl of stew and brings it to Roosevelt with an eating utensil.

"Mystery stew tonight, Doctor. Enjoy."

She looks up at the burly chef questioningly.

"What's the mystery?"

Butch cracks an easy smile, returning to the cook station.

"If'n you'll enjoy it or not."

She tips her bowl toward the firelight and picks at a random chunk of sinewy meat. Turning it over in the mix, she looks up Tusk.

"What kind of meat is this?"

"Who knows?"

Roosevelt looks over at Butch then again toward Tusk.

"I was hoping you did."

Africa Tusk

The slightly intoxicated hunter offers a shrug then tilts his head with an abstract thought as he watches her sniff the contents of the bowl.

"You know how Bushmen catch an elephant?"
The female doctor turns her inquisitiveness up from her steaming meal, interested.

"No, how's that?"

"They dig a big, wide hole and fill it with bundles of dry sticks, grass and branches."
Tusk takes a brief sipping drink from his tin cup while remaining bizarrely serious in his storytelling.

"They light the whole thing on fire and let it burn down for many days."

Roosevelt absentmindedly stirs the contents of the steaming stew as she listens.

"What's the purpose of that?"

"After the flames have all died down and the heat is mostly gone, an elephant will walk up to that hole and peer down over the edge."
Shifting the hot bowl in her lap, Roosevelt leans forward in her chair intrigued.

"Then what? How do they catch the elephant?"
Tusk takes a long, extended slug from his tin cup and lowers the vessel to reveal a smart grin.

"They sneak up and kick 'em in the ash-hole."

A spoonful of stew raised midway to her mouth, Roosevelt pauses and turns to Butch who stifles a laugh. She turns back to Tusk and rattles her head in disbelief.

"Is that some kind of local warning lore or are you completely inebriated?"
Tusk snorts and crosses an ankle over his knee.

"Just their way of doin' things … eat up, we have another long day of travel tomorrow."

"How many more days until the border region?"

The safari hunter sips the dark contents from the cup in hand and looks up to the star-filled sky.

"Probably two more days if we don't hit any delays or get bogged down with miscellaneous items."

"Does that refer to my gear?"

"Yes, it does."

The lady doctor studies the man in the chair across from her as he gazes into the starry heavens.

"I won't slow us down any."

"We'll see ..."

Roosevelt finally lifts the spoonful of stew to her lips, blows on it and eats. She chews, swallows and gives a saluting gesture toward Butch which he returns with a slight bow while ladling another serving into a bowl.

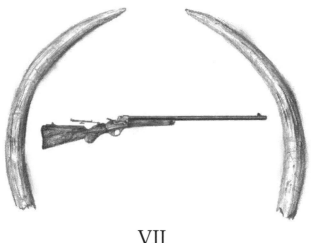

VII

The purple light before daybreak glows into the interior of the tent canvas walls. There is a quiet tap on the flap door and Tusk rouses from a light wakening sleep and brushes the back of his hand across his cheek.

"What is it?"

Mogambo peeks in with a grim expression on his face.

"Bwana, we spot Digger trucks three kilometers south, trailing small herd."

Tusk leaps from the wood framed cot, already dressed in his britches and pulls his tall leather boots on.

"Ready the jeep with our gear. Tell Butch to keep the woman here. I'll be ready in five."

The sun begins to peek over the horizon and blaze through the brushy landscape. At the wheel of the Willys Jeep, Tusk drives with Mogambo seated beside.

The gun bearer holds a collection of rifles alongside his knee as the all-terrain vehicle bounces and roars over dry, sunbaked grasses, leaving a wake of dust and awakened wildlife in the early morning glow.

Staring ahead, Mogambo points to another trail of dust on the distant horizon and Tusk nods grimly. He cuts the wheel and runs their path parallel to the barely visible procession of trucks. The sun starts to shine golden on the world around them and Tusk jams his booted foot on the gas pedal and roars the jeep forward toward the intended target.

On a sloped hillside behind the cover of tall grass and scrub bush, Tusk and Mogambo conceal themselves. They watch through field glasses as the small convoy of trucks assembles just beyond the herd of elephants. Tusk lowers the binoculars, wipes his eyes of dirt and raises the distance glasses again.

"It looks to be Digger men again."

Mogambo sits watching, stock still, with a bolt-action, scoped rifle cradled across his lap.

"We not too late. We get closer, Bwana?"

With a slight shake of his head, Tusk continues to study the movements of the men and trucks.

"I don't see any guns yet. We'll wait."

Under the increasing temperatures of day, Tusk and Mogambo lie in wait on the small hillside watching the men at the trucks. The suspicious looking crowd stands around and smokes, seeming to wait anxiously for a late arrival as they watch the small herd of tuskers graze in the distance.

Africa Tusk

The thick morning air begins to thump with an increasing flutter of sound as something pounds the humid breeze. The men loafing around the trucks spring to life and Tusk observes a flurry of activity through the binoculars. Mogambo raises the rifle scope to his eye and scans the area down below. His ear to the wind, Tusk listens to the reverberations as the heavy thumping nears and the sound of a rotator engine grows louder.

The men near the trucks respond to handheld radios and load up as if to flee. Tusk lowers his field glasses and looks over to Mogambo lying in the grass, peering through his scope with the rifle at his shoulder.

"Do Park Rangers in this district have choppers available to patrol lands out here?"

"No, Bwana ..."

Tusk raises the field glasses again and spots a military helicopter as it flies low over the tree-line, coming in fast.

"Who the hell is that, then?"

The herd of elephants sense danger and fan their large ears to the sky and trumpet sounds of warning. The thumping sound of the approaching helicopter is momentarily drowned out by the thundering stampede of elephants fleeing the area. The trucks fire up their engines and start after the elephant herd as the helicopter flies low overhead. Mogambo perches himself up on his elbows and watches the hectic scene.

"What we do now, Bwana?"

Tusk watches through the field glasses and tries to make sense of the unusual situation.

"I can't tell what is going on down there!"

Suddenly a side-panel door on the helicopter slides open and a burst of machine gun fire kicks up earthen divots amidst the fleeing elephants. A barrage of bullets from the sky tears into the herd and one of the larger bulls tumbles to his knees. The other members of the elephant family unit circle around to come to his aid and the dark menacing helicopter hovers above.

Mogambo clicks off the safety on the bolt-action rifle and puts his eye to the sighted scope.

"Them's poachers, Bwana!"

A swell of rage envelops Tusk as he tosses aside his field glasses and grabs up his long-range hunting rifle. He presses the worn wooden stock of the Remington Rolling Block to his shoulder, takes aim at the attacking helicopter and leads it across the sky.

The trigger squeezes back and the large caliber lead projectile crashes into the man working the machine gun inside the helicopter bay door. Tusk slams open the smoking breach of the Rolling Block rifle, ejects the spent brass cartridge and slides in another finger-sized load from the ammo sleeve on his vest.

"Make every round count! Once they locate our position, we're sitting ducks."

Mogambo fixes his scope crosshairs on the chopper and lets off a round that skitters off the glass front cockpit.

"Bullet no damage glass in front, Bwana."

"Yeah, I see that …"

The ominous helicopter lifts and swings away from the panicked elephant herd, rerouting its course. The injured door gunner is hastily tossed out from the gaping side panel and tumbles to the ground below.

Africa Tusk

Another figure steps into the gunner position at the open bay of the chopper and heavy machine gun fire rips up the hillside in the direction of Tusk and Mogambo.

Lining up the sights on the long octagonal barrel, Tusk sends another shot into the gunner position at the side bay of the aircraft. The door-mounted weapon violently swings upward and to the side, knocking the man behind into the aircraft. The helicopter tilts forward and keeps coming on as militia clad figures appear at each side of the chopper with automatic rifles in hand. Mogambo fires off another shot which sparks off the upper cockpit, then looks over at Tusk.

"No good, Bwana. They gonna be on us soon."

Tusk reloads again and glances down to the men by the trucks as they take out their supply of automatic weapons. The sharp retort of gunfire ensues and the poachers begin to unleash the lethal firearms on the shielding elephants along the perimeter of the herd.

"Aim for the blades and disable the rotary."
Mogambo snaps off several ineffective shots at the helicopter's top rotor. The attacking aircraft bears down on their position and Tusk waits patiently with careful aim while Mogambo provides cover fire.

Almost on top of them, the hovering war-bird turns broadside to give the door gunner at the side bay position a shooting advantage. As machine gun fire showers around them, Tusk puts a shot directly into the helicopter's tail rotor. The large caliber bullet smashes through the turning blade and the chopper retreats in a slow descending spin with a damaged tail mechanism.

In a squeal of grinding metal, the military style helicopter does several full rotations and spirals to the ground for a rough landing. Men in camo attire tumble from the landed craft and scurry away from the whirling top rotor. Tusk and Mogambo return their focus to the hostile attack on the elephant herd and wince at the vile destruction of wildlife.

Mogambo fires a shot to gauge distance to the faraway poachers but comes up short.

"Them's too far out of range. We move in?"

"We've got no advantage on them now. They'll turn on us and we won't have a chance."

The native gun bearer lowers his rifle grimly as the pop of machine gun fire erupts undeterred. They watch as one of the armed figures below suspiciously spins and tumbles forward.

"You see that chief?"

Tusk brings the field glasses to his eyes and murmurs.

"Yeah, did one of them cause an accident?"

The professional hunter watches through the distance glasses as panic sets in below. Coming from an unidentified source, another gun-wielding poacher is inflicted with a mortal gunshot wound to the chest. Tusk and Mogambo watch in amazed curiosity as the illegal hunters scramble for the trucks under sporadic but lethal gunfire.

The murderous attack that was once on the elephant herd is now turned on the fleeing poachers. Several men run from the now idle helicopter only to be cut down by successive strikes of gunfire. The ghastly moan of dying elephants echoes across the valley as Tusk surveys the scene, slightly taken aback.

"Where's it coming from?"

"The sky is angry, Bwana …"

Mogambo scans the valley all around and finally locates a flashing of light near a vehicle on the extreme far horizon behind them. A faint buzzing sound, like a hive of bees, catches Tusk's attention and he looks skyward. He squints into the midday sun and identifies a remotely controlled aerial device hovering high over the valley. As if on cue, both the men point in opposing directions; Tusk skyward to the observing drone and Mogambo to the faraway support vehicle.

"Up there!"

"Over here, Bwana!"

The two look to the other questioningly then to where each man gestures. Tusk makes an assessment of the drone overhead then looks to the solitary operation set far apart from everything else. Instinctively knowing the answer already, Tusk mutters aloud.

"Whose vehicle is that?"

The invisible battle continues as casualties are inflicted from the unseen source. Mogambo looks up to the drone aerial and down at the ivory poachers as they are systematically gunned down in their tracks. From the far-off hillside, they observe as one of the trucks is able to get clear of the area with three survivors inside. The disabled helicopter and an abandoned support truck sit motionless on the grisly site littered with discarded firearms and the bodies of assassinated poachers strewn about among the decimated elephants.

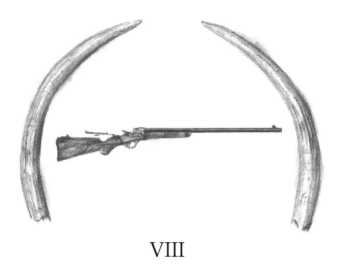

VIII

The Willys Jeep drives at a swift pace toward the distant parked vehicle. Tusk has his .45 auto sidearm laid across his lap and Mogambo holds the scoped rifle at the ready. As the jeep moves nearer, Tusk removes his foot from the gas pedal, taps the shifter into neutral and lets the idling jeep roll to a stop.

He reaches next to his seat for field glasses and studies the setup across the distance.

"Goddammit ... That's our truck."

Mogambo peers over at him with a peculiar grimace and Tusk jams the jeep's shifter back into gear. He pounds his foot on the gas and sends up a rooster-tail of dirt and grass debris from the rear tire.

The open-top jeep pulls up to the safari truck and skids sideways to a halt. A cloud of dust settles over the vehicle as Tusk sits behind the wheel, staring at Butch and Roosevelt standing nearby. The jeep's engine finally clatters to a stop and Tusk steps out with Mogambo.

The rescued pair stands before the two in front of the supply truck. There is silence until Tusk growls low.

"What the hell is going on?"

The tension is thick as Tusk follows Butch's gaze over to a futuristic looking gun on a tripod and the wirelessly attached computer monitor in the lady doctor's hands.

Roosevelt taps a few buttons on the control pad and looks up at Tusk. Her grave demeanor is almost as sour looking as his.

"Thanks for waking me, Mister Kalispell."

Tusk marches over, holding his pistol at his side and stops before her, angry, confused and frustrated.

"Waking you! Why in blazes are you even out here and what is this damned thing?"

She lowers the controller and stares unruffled at Tusk.

"This is the future of anti-poaching."

Tusk looks down to the keypad and monitor in her hand then to the electronic controlled weaponry.

"A god-damned computer?"

"It saved your ass."

The enraged hunter looks to his associate Butch but only receives an empty shrug of innocence. Tusk waves his arm toward the scene of the massacre.

"That was all your doings out there?"

"Not all of it. You shot down the helicopter."

Roosevelt smirks as she holds out the controller attached to the monitor and ushers Tusk closer.

"Have a look for yourself."

Eric H. Heisner

Tusk steps up and Roosevelt turns the display to show him the aerial view of the dead poachers and the surrounding carnage.

"I see it on there and I saw it yonder, but how did that thing in the sky take down all those men?"
Roosevelt adjusts the flight controls and the aerial drone zooms in with a targeting apparatus on the screen.

"It didn't. The drone puts a virtual bull's eye on each ... uh, objective and this thing ..."
The weapon rotates almost silently as the targeting is selected. Roosevelt takes a few steps over and places her hand on the assemblage of hi-tech looking machinery.

"This technology can shoot over four kilometers."

Tusk scans his eyes over the complicated weapon pairing of computer and long distance cannon.

"Not very intimate."
Roosevelt turns and gives Tusk a peculiarly interested expression. There is some hint of surprise to her voice in reaction to his sensitive comment on death.

"How so?"

"Who takes responsibility?"

"For what?"

"The lives it snuffs out."

"I can program the drone to fly anywhere in range and to select targets on visual contact."

She moves her hand around the touchpad and the graphics on the screen change perspective. Zooming across blurring terrain, the visuals come to a standstill with Tusk's parked jeep in view on the display monitor. The target locks and flashes red. Tusk looks at his jeep and up to the drone high above in the sky.

"Don't you dare shoot my Willys!"

He turns to the computerized weapon on the tripod as it readjusts and aims the business end skyward. Roosevelt taps a series of short commands on the controller and the flashing red target image switches off.

"Like I said, it can lock into any target selected." Tusk turns his attention again to Butch and receives no supportive response from the quiet accomplice. He looks back at Roosevelt and shakes his head.

"I assume the only spot in the territory that's safe from that thing is where you're standing?"

"Yes, I guess you could say that."

Bottled up with a conflicted rage, Tusk continues to hold the cocked pistol at his side as he paces around the computer weaponized technology.

"So, what's the grim future look like? These all-seeing computer cannons posted like guard towers? No person, place or thing safe from its reaches?"
Roosevelt watches the professional hunter in his agitated state and considers her answer carefully.

"To start, maybe just a few at the borders."
He stops his circling and faces off to Roosevelt.

"To start?"

"Yes, in troubled areas."
Tusk regards her with a deep penetrating stare.

"Troubled areas? Like where the Rangers keep getting killed or where the animals are most hunted?

"Yes, those would be considered trouble areas."

"Depending on who is doing the considering, somewhere along the line my ranch might be a tangible target for one of them."

Tusk engages the safety action on the handgun, puts it aside under the seat in the jeep then looks up to the aerial drone hovering high above, nearly soundless. Roosevelt remains respectfully observant as the cynical hunter marches around the assembly of weaponized machinery and continues to let the shock of the new technology sink in. He moves slowly and studies the components of the futuristic setup.

"What about that helicopter we saw today?"

"Yes."

"What do you mean, *Yes*?"

Tusk turns his shoulder toward the others and faces Roosevelt as she responds with a cool casualness.

"Yes, it could have taken it out of commission if you hadn't already damaged the tail rotor."

"You saw all that?"

"We saw two chumps lying in the tall grass, helpless to save any animals, out-gunned and about to make a last stand."

A feeling of embarrassment washes over Tusk as he steps away and glances over to Butch who waits by the truck, quietly observing. The thought of his friend seeing him in a compromised situation burns into his pride and self-confidence. He ponders the circumstances a short moment then turns and stares at the advanced technological weapon again.

"Well Doctor, you missed two of those poachers who drove away in the truck."

Roosevelt stares over at him stone-faced.

"It doesn't miss. There were three in the truck."

Africa Tusk

Tusk looks to his old pal, Butch again but gets nothing. The burly cook and safari guide casts his gaze to the ground and toes a clump of dirt with his boot. Roosevelt clears her throat and continues.

"Unlike your primitive method to deter poachers, part of this very expensive mechanism's work is done through unseen intimidation and the effects of folklore."

The computerized gun quietly readjusts again, but continues to point skyward. Tusk and Butch exchange a knowing glance but the guide partner remains silent. The heat of the late morning hangs heavy under the rising sun as Tusk walks over to his jeep. He puts a foot on the side rail and offers an acquiescent nod.

"Well, there's a lot to be said for legends."

Tusk peers skyward again as the drone hovers overhead in the clear, cloudless sky.

"Are we finished here?"

Roosevelt nods and lowers the handheld computer.

"Yes, I think so."

"Good, then Butch will help you get it packed up. Let's get away from this place before the Rangers or Military decide to make a showing."

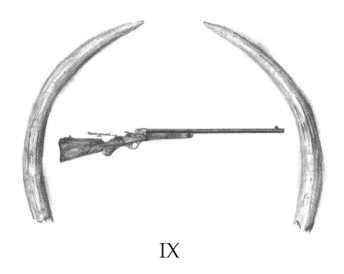

IX

A convoy led by Tusk's vehicle and the two following support trucks rumbles along the dry African terrain. The midday sun beats down as Tusk drives the jeep with Roosevelt seated beside. She gazes around as he stares grimly forward and occasionally swings the steering wheel to avoid a cavernous dip in their path.

Traveling along the unmarked trail, a hard bump of the tires jostles them from their seats. Tusk adjusts his hat and continues to stare silent at the path before them. Roosevelt watches Tusk's attentive steering a while before clearing her throat with a guilt-ridden cough.

"Sorry I lied about what I do …"

Tusk glances over at her briefly, continuing to drive, his hard expression unchanged.

"I knew you were lying …"

"You did?"

Africa Tusk

"I've met women before."

Roosevelt swallows the insult to her gender.

"Did you know I was part of a NGO?"

"No ... but there's always something."

The safari hunter takes one hand off the steering wheel, rubs his thigh and lets the jeep coast a bit. He turns to the doctor seated next to him and looks her over from head to toe with a grimace.

"You're awfully well put together for a doctor."

"I'm part of a non-governmental organization for International Anti-Poaching and Trafficking."

Tusk puts both hands back to the task of steering the jeep and smirks toward her.

"That's quite a mouthful."

"I'm in the Ivory division."

"Does it say all that on your business card?"

The female doctor grips her hand alongside the seat to keep from bouncing out through the cut-away jeep door. Roosevelt shakes her head negative as she looks around at the scenic wildlife environs unpopulated by people. She speaks just above the engine noise.

"There is nothing on the books ... no business card, no company records and no public relations."

"You're kind of like a spook?"

"I'm working out of the U.K. branch in London."

"And you want me to help you set this thing up somewhere down here in my backyard?"

The convoy scatters a gathering of zebras ahead and Roosevelt watches Tusk peer over his shoulder at the following safari trucks. Roosevelt realizes the delicate nature of her position and tries to appeal to Tusk's conservationist mentality.

"At the current rate of ivory poaching, the African elephant will be extinct in only a few years. We need you, Mister Kalispell … to help us test this anti-poaching technology in the field."

He turns and sneers with a morbid tinge to his manner.

"Didn't you just do that back there?"

"That wasn't the optimal situation."

"It never is."

Roosevelt puts her hand to the edge of the upright windscreen and looks back at the rumbling trucks behind. She turns with a pleading stare at Tusk.

"Will you help us?"

"Why me?"

"You have knowledge of Africa's wildlife."

"There are plenty of local safari guides and wealthy animal rights groups that would be more than pleased to show you the sights."

The jeep bounces her in the passenger seat and Roosevelt chooses her words carefully.

"Mister Kalispell … you have a certain reputation for anti-poaching and proactive implementation that we thought might fit with our specific ideals and mission."

He looks at her, not sure if he should feel insulted or not.

"Reputation, huh?"

"From what we've heard from reliable sources is you're not one to wait on the inefficiency of government or international policy to do what needs doing. You have a certain self-reliance, moral standing and primal outlook on mankind's responsibilities to protect the continuation of a species and wildlife."

Tusk continues to drive the jeep ahead at a bone-jarring speed and shrugs his shoulders with empathy. He glances over at her and his forehead crinkles beneath the brim of his wide-brimmed hat.

"I don't know about moral standing, but I do have a sense of fair-play which those bastard poachers and their illegal ivory trade rub the wrong way."

"That's why we need you. These people have to be stopped and the ivory theft put to an end."
The pair in the jeep continues to bounce along the grassy pastureland inhabited by grazing wildlife all around. Tusk nods his reluctant agreement.

"It didn't used to be like this."

"What didn't?"

"Africa ... and the rest of the world."
Roosevelt sits watching Tusk drive and he continues.

"Not so many years ago, hunting was a part of everyday life and a noble profession. It's this killer mentality with no regard for consequence that has made hunting, guns and shooting all ugly words."

"It's the times we live in, Mister Kalispell."

Behind the wheel of the jeep, Tusk mentally reflects back on the stories of his grandfather and the modest rural lifestyle he grew up loving. He takes his eyes from the path and looks over at Roosevelt.

"You can drop the Mister Kalispell stuff and call me Tusk ... and why don't you just say what it is?"

"What would you name the program?"
Tusk pauses a moment before speaking.

"A drone-guided, electro … I don't know."

"Anti-poaching tech pretty much covers it."

The two bob and sway in the vehicle while silently staring forward. Tusk ponders the unintended consequences of the anti-poaching weapon's use a moment before resuming the conversation.

"If this happens to work in the most dangerous areas of the region successfully, what would ensure that you don't turn this new weapon on folks like me who professionally hunt game for our livelihood?"

"What if I said you could trust us?"

Tusk blurts out a laugh.

"You already lied to me about what you're doing here and who you are. Trust you? You could be from one of those animal rights groups that think cows have emotions, pigs should be clean and chickens deserve homes better than their keepers."

"I'm here for the elephants."

The jeep idles and rolls to a stop, looking out over a sharp ravine which drops off in front of them.

"Once you set up 'Big Brother', there is no getting him out of your life. Whoever is in control of this thing will be a lot like government. It is as good or bad as the ones running it. They'll take your freedoms away but never give any back."

Roosevelt nods her agreement and stares over the escarpment to the protected valley below.

"Don't you think some drastic measures are needed to ensure the survival of a species?"

Tusk looks to Roosevelt with a grim expression.

"This may or may not be the way to do it."

Africa Tusk

"Do you have another?"

"There is always another way, good or bad."

They stare out over the wide ravine and hear, carried through the wind, the haunting trumpets of herding elephants. Tusk takes a deep breath and with one hand on the wheel the other drops to the knobbed gear shifter.

"I'll help you against the poachers … but I hope we won't end up in each other's target sights one day."

Roosevelt nods somberly and Tusk sharply cranks the wheel on the jeep. He grinds the shifter, eases off the clutch and pushes his boot on the gas pedal. The jeep turns and drives away from the deep chasm in the unknown path ahead.

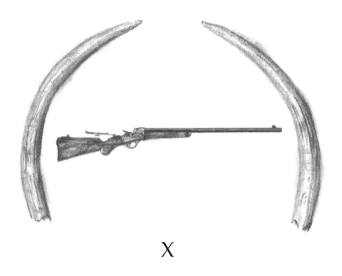

X

The African wilderness comes alive in the dimness of evening with calling sounds from creatures on the hunt and clicking insects. Safari trucks are parked and the camp structures are being set up. Tusk stands at the edge of the activity, peering out into the night, smoking a cigar. He takes a puff from the stout wand of tobacco and sends a ringed cloud of smoke skyward.

The fire at the center of camp burns brightly as Tusk observes from a distance Butch chatting quietly with Roosevelt. He watches them keenly as they sip beverages from tin vessels and seem to be bonding over shared stories. At the edge of darkness, the light from the campfire catches Tusk's features and casts him in silhouette against the night. He waits awhile before walking over to join them at the fire pit.

Africa Tusk

Tusk stares down at the rolling flames consuming the found timber and takes another drag from his cigar. Silence ensues as the two chatting individuals seated in creaking canvas camp chairs shift positons and pause their conversation. Roosevelt glances up at Tusk and remains quiet until Butch breaks the stillness.

"Rosie here was just telling me about some of her work in India with tigers before switching divisions."

Tusk nods and puffs at the cigar. He lets the cloud of smoke waft over him in the flickering glow of the campfire. His eyes dart over to the lady doctor with a curious suspicion while he rolls the shortened tobacco between his thumb and finger.

"Doctor Roosevelt Hamilton Adams ... three American presidents?"

She looks up at him and sits back in her chair jauntily.

"Two actually, Hamilton wasn't a president."

"Humph."

"Do you have a snide comment to follow?"

"Is that your real name?"

"Would I make something like that up?"

Tusk looks away from her and raises the cigar to his mouth. He takes a short drag and clenches the soft end of the tobacco roll between his teeth.

"What's the deal with your folks?

Roosevelt stares across the fire at him straight-faced.

"I have a brother named Jackson Kennedy and a sister, Carter Taft."

Butch nearly spits his drink as he lowers his tin cup.

"That's rich, really?"

She turns to Butch and offers a sweet smile as he wipes the dribble off his chin with his shirt sleeve.

"No, but Mister Tusk would like to believe that." Tusk chews on the cigar a moment then grumbles as he talks through his teeth.

"Are your folks kind of nutty for presidents?"

"My mother was a Texan and my father was Brit who taught American History and Insight at Oxford." Butch shifts in his chair and nods.

"Smart guy, huh?"

"Both my parents were."

The campfire crackles and Butch looks up at Tusk as he stands in the broken firelight thoughtfully chewing on his cigar. The burly safari hunter watches his partner exhale a cloud of smoke and tilts his head to Roosevelt sitting next to him.

"You made up yer mind yet if we're gonna help her set up that anti-poaching contraption?

The hard shadows of Tusk's features acknowledge Butch, then turn to address Roosevelt.

"We're about a day's travel from the border territory. There is plenty of illegal activity there. We'll have to be very careful from here on out."

Butch grins in the darkness, offers up his raised tin cup in a toasting fashion before he takes a swig.

"I told you he'd come around Missus."

Tusk turns back to Butch and tosses the remnants of his cigar into the dancing flames of the campfire.

"Suppose you're on her side of it now?"

"Jest heard her out and saw a bit of sense to it."

Africa Tusk

Roosevelt sits back attentive as Tusk stands lighted in the glow of the jumping flames and paces before the campfire, speaking clear and direct.

"It's a dangerous and slippery slope to have someone watch you from afar … in the crosshairs with their finger on the trigger."

Butch fondles the cup in hand and speaks thoughtful.

"We can't do it all ourselves, pal. From personal experience, it really could deter a lot of them poachers."

Tusk nods and shoots a stern gaze to the lady doctor.

"We'll see how it goes."

The broad-shouldered, safari mate shifts in his camp chair and turns to face Roosevelt. Butch hooks his oversized thumb toward Tusk and grins widely.

"Savin' his bacon should give ya some mileage."

She returns the smile, angling her attention toward Tusk.

"It's always nice to test equipment in the field."

Tusk glares at Butch, then over at Roosevelt. With her long hair pulled over one shoulder glistening in the flickering light, she looks almost angelic. He tilts his head warningly.

"The playing field is about to get substantially more treacherous. We'll be testing a whole lot more than your technology."

He gives an ill-tempered grunt, toes an errant spark from the campfire with his boot and walks away into the darkness. A warm southern breeze flutters the tent canvas and the fire wavers in response. Roosevelt sits in uncertain repose by the flickering light of the flames and looks over at Butch.

"I don't think he likes me very much."

"Most folks get that same impression. He'll come 'round … or he won't."

The noises coming from nightfall in the African bush are loud and raucous. Insects chatter with shrill calls and nighttime prowlers send howls and guttural growls across the dark landscape. The distant glow of unobstructed stars in the sky above, only amplify the shadows of the unseen nocturnal activity.

The canvas safari tents sit assembled around the dying embers of the pit-fire from the evening prior. A dim glow reflects on the fabric dwellings from the light of the rising moon. Inside one of the tents, Tusk rolls over on his low slung canvas cot and his eyes blink open, still half-asleep. Suddenly, he bolts up and listens to the dark silence all around.

The radiance of moonlight shines through the travel-stained tent covering and illuminates Roosevelt as she sleeps. A stealthy hand reaches from the shadows to cover over her mouth and clamps down tight. She is awkwardly jostled from sleep as a familiar voice rasps in a hushed tone near her ear.

"Keep quiet …"

Her wide-alert eyes roll over toward the shadowed figure of Tusk and she hastily peels his hand from her face.

"What the hell are you doing?"

"Listen!"

Roosevelt pushes up to an elbow and perks her ears to the lingering silence outside.

"I don't hear anything."

Africa Tusk

Tusk silently nods at her knowingly.

"Yeah, I don't either."

The lady doctor sits up further and conceals her sparsely clad torso in the dim moonlight. She looks over at Tusk squatted next to her bed shirtless in only his britches, boots and Stetson hat. He has a pistol tucked at his waist and his long barreled sport rifle in hand.

"What's going on?"

"I don't know yet."

"Where's your shirt?"

The alert hunter shakes his head annoyed and puts a shushing finger to his lips. A lone cackle of a hyena pierces the night and fades away. They both listen into the deafening silence until the soft crunching sound of feet on dry grass happens outside the tent.

Tusk and Roosevelt follow the sound of the quiet steps as they move around to the front door flap. On his haunches, Tusk creeps toward the front entrance, adjusts the pistol in his waistband and waits with the rifle held across his bare chest. Slowly the tent flap opens from the outside and Tusk instantly jams the rifle butt through the opening into the face of the unsuspecting visitor.

Following the solid crack of walnut gunstock to human skull, there is a surprised howl of pain as the intruder stumbles backward into the quiet camp. Tusk grabs Roosevelt by the arm and urges her to the back of the tent. He lifts the canvas side and ushers her under.

"Hurry ... Out!"

She gives him a single panicked glance, grabs her shirt and slides under the raised tent wall.

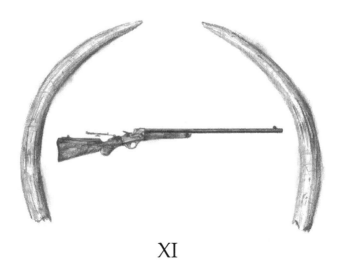

XI

The brief tranquility of night is broken and the campsite is suddenly alive with a frenzy of commotion. Blinding bursts of light from the muzzle flash of automatic rifles erupts into the darkness and rips through the assembly of tents and vehicles. Loud commanding barks, in native tongue add tension to the hostile attack on the camp.

Outside the canvas shelter, Roosevelt looks around into the confusion and Tusk appears quickly at her side. He pulls her away from the circle of tents and into the nearby shelter of darkness. She looks behind at the multiple flashes of gunfire in the camp and stammers as Tusk ushers her along in to the bush.

"Where are we going?"

"Move quick and stay low."

"What's happening back there?"

"It's a raid."

Africa Tusk

The glimmering dark, upright form of a man rushes past them and Roosevelt lets out a surprised yelp. Tusk raises his pistol and the soft baritone voice of Mogambo whispers from the night.

"Mister Tusk ... Bwana."

Roosevelt tries to make out the features of the gun bearer in the dark shadows but the flashing glimmer of his eyes is all she can identify.

"Mogambo?"

"Yes, Memsahib."

Dressed only in dark shorts and trail boots, Mogambo emerges from the night with Tusk's alternate double rifle in hand and looks apologetically to his employer.

"I am sorry, Bwana ... I was to get her and she was already gone."

"No worries, let's get to cover."

The prattling sounds of night creatures remain at bay as the intermittent burst of gunfire lights up the overrun campsite. Roosevelt sits crouched next to Tusk and Mogambo, sheltered in the brush a good distance from the unexpected raid. She rubs the sleep from her eyes and lets them adjust to the moonlight.

"What about the others?"

The whites of the gun bearer's eyes flash over to her.

"Everybody up and get out quick."

"What do they want?"

The soft click of a handgun's safety mechanism being engaged is muted in Tusk's hand as he pushes his pistol back into his waistband.

"They're looting our gear and food supplies now. The show of firepower is to keep us away."

Roosevelt keeps her voice low and whispers.

"Looting? What kind of raid is this?"

Tusk glances over at her in the dark, noticing her white tank-top nearly glowing in the night.

"Mostly they take all the food, guns and ammo they can carry. I've installed kill switches on all the vehicle's fuel lines which are engaged when parked."

The repetitive cranking sound of the trucks trying to turn over resonates from the camp and Roosevelt shakes her head at Tusk.

"This has happened before?"

"Yeah, occasionally. If they can't take the trucks, it greatly limits what they can carry away. It makes them easier to track too if we need to steal stuff back."

She stares at him disbelievingly and he grimaces at her surprise in the dimness. Huddled in the bush, Tusk watches the camp and whispers.

"What the hell did you think I meant when I said it was dangerous out here? The snakes and critters that would like to eat you are the least of your problems when you're surrounded by extreme poverty and a corrupt government."

The flashing light of gunfire shimmers off Roosevelt's features as she glares at Tusk.

"What about *my* gear?"

"These people wouldn't know what to do with a bunch of computers and techno garbage. When you're hungry, the last thing you need is a toy helicopter."

Africa Tusk

In the background, a truck's engine fires up followed shortly by the sound of the jeep starting. Tusk turns to Mogambo and they both peer out as beams of headlights appear in the now mobile camp. Mogambo is taken aback and blinks his eyes, staring forward.

"Bwana ... these may not be our usual raiders."

"Dammit!"

Roosevelt watches as the lights swing through the ravaged camp and prepare to drive off.

"What's going on, now?"

Tusk drops down from his haunches and rests his rifle across his thigh. His features turn hard as he watches helplessly the distant activity in the camp.

"They started the trucks and will clean us out."

"My gear too?"

"Everything worth taking."

She stares at him and rasps in a loud whisper.

"And what are you going to do about it?"

The rumble of engines and the lights of vehicles cut through the night. Tusk turns to looks at his lady client with mounting frustration but tempers his anger.

"Not a damned thing at the moment!"

"My equipment is worth millions."

"How much is your life worth?"

The three watch from cover as the lights of the trucks pull away and drive into the moonlit distance.

Several hours later, the chill of morning comes on as moisture rises up from the grasses and the sky shows hints of daylight, just before sunrise. Tusk huddles his knees for warmth against his shirtless torso. He climbs to his feet, stretches and nudges Roosevelt with the side of his boot. Lying curled on the ground, she rouses from her restless sleep and murmurs.

"What is it?"

Tusk grabs up his long barreled rifle and belt of ammunition. He motions toward a dark, half-dressed figure jogging in their direction from the encampment.

"Mogambo scouted the area and it's in the clear." Roosevelt climbs to her feet and looks out across the open grassland toward their plundered campsite.

"They left the tents?"

"They have no need of 'em. C'mon, let's go."

A good distance from the campsite, Tusk leads Roosevelt out of the concealing brush toward the few scattered items left behind. She looks to where the truck was parked with her gear and only the trampled grass and empty tire tracks remain. Mogambo nods toward Tusk and veers off to search for any remnants of supplies missed in the night raid.

Cursing under his breath, Tusk peers inside a half-collapsed tent and kicks the remaining support pole aside. The canvas shell floats to the ground and slowly deflates in a shallow heap. The bullet-riddled campsite is a scattered mix of various tossed supplies. Roosevelt steps over to look inside her canvas dwelling and comes out flabbergasted.

"Everything is gone."

She casts her disbelieving gaze around the broken remnants of tents and shakes her head.

Africa Tusk

Nearby, Mogambo looks out to the wild surroundings as Tusk stands in a set of tire tracks and stares off in the direction of travel. The native man points his arm and extends a finger.

"Bwana …"

Tusk turns and follows Mogambo's motion. From the faraway brush appear several of their native crewmen, following along behind Butch.

Rifle cradled over his shoulder, Butch wears a hang-dog look as he strides toward camp, his gaze connecting with Tusk. He stops a short distance away, speaks Swahili over his shoulder to the crew and dismisses them to gather up whatever items to be found. The broad-chested safari hunter walks closer and offers a pathetic smile toward Roosevelt and Mogambo.

"I don't understand how they figured out the kill switch on the trucks…"

Tusk turns away and continues to look out into the distance. The empty horizon shows no sign of the stolen vehicles, except the faint mash of tire tread upon the long expanse of grassy ground.

"Everyone accounted for?"

"Yeah, they all cleared out unhurt."

Tusk holds his rifle, picks up a shirt from over a fallen chair and looks to where the tire tracks lead away.

"I'm going after our vehicles. Get me two volunteers to help me drive 'em back."

Mogambo steps forward and holds his head high.

"I go with you, Bwana."

"Fine."

Butch lowers the rifle from his shoulder and hitches it on his hip.

"I'll go with ya."

"No good … I want you to make your way back to the ranch and bring extra fuel and supplies to leave for us. Besides, I need you to take her back."

Roosevelt steps forward and crosses her arms.

"I go where you go."

"Like hell, you do."

"I'm not just going away when I have millions of dollars of equipment out there in who knows hands."

Tusk exchanges a troubled glance with Butch and faces off to Roosevelt as she stands firm.

"That's the dangerous part. We don't know exactly who they are."

Butch scans the pillaged camp as the crewmen wrap up flattened tents and various articles from the departed trucks. He turns to Tusk questioningly.

"Uh pal … who do you think it might be?"

Tusk pulls on his shirt and buttons it up the center.

"News travels fast out here in the bush. My thoughts are word got out about her mystery weapon."

Tusk and Butch both turn to stare at Roosevelt who returns their earnest glares with a sheepish smile.

"Do you believe those men we allowed to escape the other day are responsible?"

Butch stifles a grin and Tusk tilts his head with reproach at her mention of the event.

"*We* allowed?"

"Our studies have supported the idea that fear of the unknown is a useful tool and deterrent for most."

Africa Tusk

The hunter tucks the tails of his shirt into his trousers.

"Out here, fear is for sale cheap and if you let someone get away, you better count on them knifing you in the back around the next tree ... or while you sleep."

"What will they do with my gear?"

"Hopefully, they will destroy it."

"It's worth millions!"

Tusk smirks and leans on his rifle.

"You've mentioned that."

The camp is quiet with exception of the crew folding the tent canvas and assembling a pile of remains. Roosevelt bites her lip nervous, standing before Tusk.

"There are people out there who might use the gear from this project for a less noble cause."

Tusk shakes his head uncertain.

"I doubt they will ransom it back to us. There might already be interested buyers. If they find someone who can operate it, then we will really have problems."

"I need to go with. If you leave me behind, I'll just follow you again. I can handle myself."

The cautious outdoorsman winces over his shoulder in the direction of the stolen truck's path.

"Dammit ... I don't even know how I let you convince me to start all of this. Butch, find two drivers to accompany me and bring the trucks back."

He looks to Roosevelt who stands with her arms crossed, braced and ready to follow.

"Looks like our man Mogambo will have his hands full, baby-sitting for you."

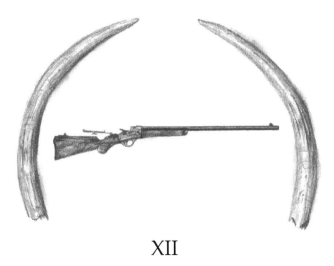

XII

The looted camp is still a disheveled mess of tossed gear and damaged crates. Butch stands near a large pile of gathered supplies and assigns loads to the walking crew. He switches his attention to the recovery party as they approach with Mogambo carrying Tusk's extra double rifle and two native drivers carrying light loads.

"How goes it boss-man?"

Tusk stands with his single-shot rolling block slung under his arm and glances back at the camp.

"We're ready to head out."

The white hunter looks around at the folded tents and supply crates stacked on the trampled grass. Butch follows his gaze and shrugs in accordance.

"We're taking what we can, but most of this stuff we'll pick up on the return."

Africa Tusk

Tusk adjusts his hold on the heavy, long-barreled rifle and nods approval.

"I trust you know what you're doing."

They both glance back at Roosevelt as she leans over to retie the lacing on her boot. Butch coughs and murmurs.

"I hope you do too."

Tusk shifts the weight on his rucksack, frowns and looks away from the attractive lady doctor. He steps alongside Butch and they stare out to where the trail of tire tracks snakes away. Tusk heaves a sigh and speaks with a lack of optimism.

"We'll follow the trucks and reconnect with you at this site in a few days' time. If waiting isn't an option, leave me sign and hide a fuel tank with food supplies."

Butch turns to his friend and extends his hand.

"You got it. See ya in a few days."

The two safari hunters shake hands and embrace shoulders, understanding it could be their last. Tusk gives Butch a friendly pat on the back and dips his chin with a knowing acceptance. Both their eyes drop toward the long-range rifle cradled in the crook of Tusk's arm. The task at hand and consequences are understood.

Adjusting his hat, Tusk steps away and raises a single finger to the sky in an offhand goodbye gesture. He marches away and follows the tire depressions on the open ground. Over his shoulder, he calls out just loud enough the catch the breeze.

"Good Luck to ya, Butchie."

"And to you, Tusk ..."

Standing under the blazing late morning sun, Roosevelt watches the manly exchange and senses that she has witnessed rarely seen sentiments displayed by these men of action. She adjusts the load on her back and gives Butch a wave before following after Tusk in the direction of the lost vehicles. Mogambo offers a raised palm to Butch and follows diligently after his female charge with the two drivers, toting bolt-action rifles, at his heels. The small retrieval crew walks off in a single file line to the west with the cloudless light of day shining upon their shoulders.

The swift treading of white hunter boots and native sandaled feet in the waist-high grasses of the savannah go on for several miles. A metronome type huff is heard from the drivers as they lug their burden. Tusk strides at a brisk gait, ever watchful and observant of the surrounding terrain and natural sounds.

Exhausted, yet determined to keep up, Roosevelt trails behind and tries to match the enduring fleetness of the marching group. She stares ahead at the bobbing pair of packs of the two drivers and stumbles in their wake. Her assigned native protector empathetically pauses and stops to wait for her. Mogambo glistens with sweat, but seems to enjoy the fast pace.

The gun bearer smiles at Roosevelt while his alert eyes constantly scan the horizon.

"You okay, Memsahib?"

"Yes, Mogambo. Maybe just some water."

Mogambo unslings one of the water bladders from across his lean shoulders and offers her a drink. Tusk halts and looks back with a scolding gaze as she gulps a mouthful of water. Mogambo nods with understanding and tips the water vessel away.

"Not too much, Memsahib or you'll flounder."

Tusk looks up to the late afternoon sun and speaks a series of commands to his crew in Kiswahili. They nod in accordance and he returns to speaking English when he addresses Roosevelt.

"I'm going on ahead. The quicker we find them the better the chances of recovering most of our gear. Mogambo will stay with you. Keep up if you can."

She wipes the drips from her chin and stands straight.

"I'm right behind you."

Tusk grumbles his annoyance under his breath as he switches the carrying shoulder of his long gun. He adjusts the pack strap under the rifle's forestock, grips the barrel and continues on at a trotting pace. The stillness of humid air allows the sweat to pour freely as Roosevelt forces a grin and follows along behind.

The convoy of tire tracks leads to a wide twisting river alive with natural wildlife on both shores. As the band of foot travelers approaches, several large river crocodiles scamper from the tall grasses and sand banks to slide into the swift flowing current. Tusk stands with his rifle propped on his shoulder, scanning the waterway for the least perilous crossing.

The sound of rushing water swirls between the banks as Roosevelt steps up next to Tusk and Mogambo. She wipes the sweat from her cheek as she observes the submerged forms and the apprehensive walking crew standing quietly by. With hesitation she asks the looming question that hangs in the air.

"Are we going to try and swim it?"

"Some of us might not make it."

Another ten foot reptile splashes into the river and swims stealthily by. Roosevelt scans her eyes across the surface of the water and spots two more.

"Are those crocodiles?"

"Yeah, the rivers near here are full of 'em."

"Can you shoot them?"

Tusk glances over at her amused and grunts.

"Not very environmentalist of you is it? Don't have nearly enough ammunition for that sort of thing and we'd be here all day trying to keep more away."

"How will we cross to the other side?"

"We'll have to hike downriver and find some sort of bait animal to interest the crocs or makings for a raft."

"How did they get the trucks across?"

Tusk takes a knee and observes the sets of tire tracks going into the muddy water. He studies the opposite shore and lets his eyes travel downriver.

"They went in here and floated them across to that gravel embankment. The water's depth along this section is only one or two meters with a rocky shore."

The distance across the wide stream seems an easy swim with the exception of the deadly predators occupying the current. Tusk brushes the damp soil from his knee and stands. He stares across at the opposite riverbank and glances at Roosevelt.

"It may not seem like much water until you see a leathery log with a row of teeth coming at you. Their brain is smaller than your fist and a hard mark unless you're above or beside them. Even then, you don't trust a croc until it's been skinned."

He looks past his shoulder at Mogambo and the loyal native crewmen who stand by, waiting patiently.

"We'll move further down river"

Tusk repeats the command in native tongue and motions his arm toward a grouping of trees in view a distance along the river. Roosevelt notices the crew of men visually relax as the directions for the river crossing are conveyed. One of the drivers lights a cigarette and passes it to his relieved companion. Roosevelt glances back at them as she moves alongside Tusk.

"What was wrong with them?"

"They thought I was going to have 'em wade it."

"Why would they think that?"

The safari hunter continues walking as the men readjust their backpacks and follow along the riverbank.

"We've had to do it in the past."

"I thought you said we wouldn't make it?" He offers a slight grin as he strides away.

"I said *some* might not make it across. I can be a quick shot when needed and properly motivated."

She looks to the stealthy forms in the river and turns back as he marches on toward the faraway trees.

"That's what it takes to motivate you? Let's definitely do the raft building thing."

"We'll see what we come up with."

They step onto a recent animal trail created by a watering herd and walk cautiously through the thigh-high river grass. Tusk scans his eyes up the trampled path along the waterway and keeps all his senses alert.

"Be very careful through here. Crocs can smell a meal and can move quickly on land when they want to."

"Are you teasing me?"

Tusk walks swiftly, holding his rifle across his chest with his thumb pulled back on the hammer and finger inside the trigger guard.

"No ... they have very good sense for when food is around. They can grab you from cover or get you in the first seconds when you're gawking at the oversized lizard scampering toward you at lightning speed."

With boots stepping attentively in Tusk's tracks, Roosevelt looks all around into the dense grass cover.

"I'll be sure to watch where I step."

Tusk nods and points his rifle forward.

"If I say run ... move fast and don't look back."

Roosevelt nods her head in whole-hearted agreement and looks behind to the traveling crew continuing along the riverbank trail.

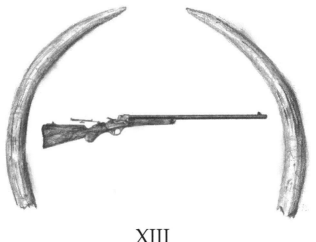

XIII

The sun burns low, nearing the horizon as Tusk picks up the foot pace. They spread out and search through tall brush and sapling trees trying to find material suitable enough for a raft. Roosevelt follows close behind Tusk and looks back at Mogambo and his crew bringing up the rear in the thick overgrown bush. The men chop long flexible shafts of vegetation and carry them over backpacks across their shoulders.

She watches the glowing sunset across the river on the horizon and moves up next to Tusk.

"Is it safe to camp next to the river?"

"We won't be stopping 'til we find those trucks."

"Who knows how far they traveled?"

Tusk halts beside the river, takes in their remote sur-roundings and watches her mop the sweat from her face.

"They came in on foot, so they can most likely be reached that way. They'll have a base camp setup."

"Well, how did they get across the river then?"
Tusk grins shrewdly at her inquiry.

"It's just a number's game."

"What?"

"One way to do it is to move everyone across at once and you'll only loose a few."

"Really?"
Tusk watches the darkening ripples swish through the water as the sunlight fades.

"I wouldn't do it with my crew since they're like family, but with your kind of people, I might risk a few."

"How about we stick with the raft idea?"

"They didn't use one ..."

His voice trails off and Roosevelt turns back from staring over her shoulder toward Mogambo and the two crewmen. She looks to Tusk questioningly.

"How do you know that?"
Tusk pushes some sapling trees aside and reveals three thick ropes stretched across the river to form a primitive sort of water crossing.

"They used a bridge."

The slacked lines stretch across the river with two tied high and a single one hanging lower. Roosevelt studies the sagging rope supports and shakes her head.

"That's not a bridge in my world."
Tusk gives a low whistle to catch his crew's attention.

"It's a Burma Bridge. They're easy to handle but hard to think about."

Africa Tusk

In the fading light of day, Roosevelt eyes the ropes with a doubtful manner and turns back as Mogambo approaches. The native gun bearer steps up with the two crewmen and smiles reassuringly.

"Is good Bwana … much quick and better."
The British doctor turns back to the three ropes again and watches as Tusk pulls on the secured end.

"Uh, Tusk … you go first, I'll follow Mogambo."
Tusk grins at her as he gives the last of the lines a tug.

"Nope, I'll follow you in case you need an extra kick in the pants to get to the other side."

The white hunter chatters in native tongue at the crew and Mogambo nods and approaches the rope bridge. He slings Tusk's double rifle across his body before gripping the two higher ropes and stepping onto the low single line. The foot line sways a bit side to side as Mogambo moves across the thick twisted twine in an agile display of balance.

The last golden rays of sunlight filter through the riverbank foliage on the opposite shore and Roosevelt holds her breath with apprehension. The lean African gun bearer nears the middle of the water crossing and the lower line sags into the swift current of the stream. Mogambo's ankles drag under the muddy rushing waters and he continues steadily across.

Mogambo nears the opposite bank and leaps to safety on the supporting tree. He deftly swings down to drop on the grassy shore before unslinging the rifle from his shoulder and waving an affirmative gesture. Tusk returns a wave of acknowledgment and gives Roosevelt a firm pat on the back.

"Okay Missy, you're next."

She stares at Tusk who mockingly curtsies and ushers her toward the rope bridge. Her eyes move to the dripping lower line near the center that dangles a few inches above the water and shakes her head, disinclined.

"What happens if I fall in?"

"You'll get wet. C'mon, before it gets dark."

"I might get eaten!"

"Possibly, it's best not to think about it."

Tusk pushes her toward the ropes and Roosevelt gets a boost from one of the native crew. She reaches up to get a firm hold on the higher lines and slowly works her way across. A momentary pause at the middle of the crossing puts the river water rushing over the ankles of her knee-high safari boots. Tusk calls to her in a loud encouraging whisper from the darkening riverbank.

"Keep moving unless you want a crocodile nibbling at the toes of your custom English boots."

The rope lines begin to bounce as Roosevelt quickens her pace with a refreshed sense of motivation. Reaching hand over hand, the bridge stretches taut with the dispersal of her weight. She arrives securely on the opposite bank and watches as one of the backpack laden drivers quickly steps up and begins the crossing.

The fading light of dusk leaves heavy shadows along the brushy shores as the last crewman takes to the Burma Bridge. The dark native hesitantly stops mid-crossing as there is a splash in the water ahead, followed quickly by the flashing report of Tusk's rifle from the darkened riverbank. Without looking below, the native continues moving his way across the suspended ropes with agile proficiency.

Aftereffects from the length of lighted muzzle-flash impede her vision as Roosevelt calls across the river to Tusk in the dimness of evening.

"Are you okay over there? What was that?"

She peers through the near darkness into the murky water at what appears to be a jam of driftwood logs floating nearby. The ominous presence of the swimming prehistoric creatures sends a chill up her spine.

Tusk speaks across the expanse of water in an unfamiliar Bantu dialect and without a word of response; Mogambo uncocks the double rifle and puts it over his shoulder. He turns Roosevelt from the water crossing and firmly escorts her from the riverbank.

"We camp a ways over there."

"What about Tusk?"

"He comes later."

"What was the shot in the river?"

"Them's crocodiles, Memsahib."

Roosevelt looks back at the shadowed obscurity of the flowing waterway as dusk is upon them.

"Then how will he get across?"

"He come later."

A partial-moon replaces the setting sun and lights the African skyline with a silvery tone. Around the cold bush camp, in the heavy shadows, nocturnal creatures begin to chatter with activity. Nightfall upon them, in the absence of firelight, Roosevelt lies against the gear pack near Mogambo and lets her eyes take in the varied shades of darkness.

The crew around her all lay in a tight grouping, fully clothed with their heads rested on piled backpacks. The soft rumbles of heavy breathing and snores come from the trail-weary men and Roosevelt closes her eyes, reluctantly succumbing to sleep.

After what seems like mere minutes, Roosevelt is suddenly pulled from her fitful slumber by a firm grasp upon her shoulder. The glistening flash of a wet hand near her face startles her awake and before she calls out, a reassuring voice whispers at her ear.

"Shh ... easy. It's me."

Roosevelt sits up relieved to make out the shimmering figure of Tusk in the moonlit darkness.

"What time is it?"

"Nighttime. We need to get moving again."

As Tusk crawls away to wake Mogambo and the others, Roosevelt can smell a distinct wetness from the river.

The native gun bearer rouses quickly without a moan of objection and awakens the crew around the cold camp. Roosevelt stares up at Tusk as he stands wet, dark and silent in a silvery silhouette against the moonlight. His long rifle perched over his shoulder and hat pushed back on his head, he looks the epitome of a competent safari figure. In a short time, the group of five is moving again, walking under expansive starlit skies.

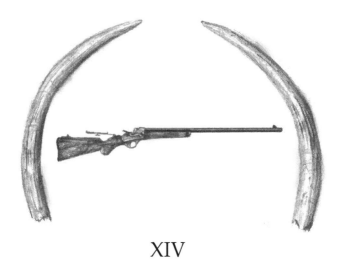

XIV

The morning sun climbs over the eastern horizon and shines brightly on the laden travelers. A faint odor of campfire smoke tinges the morning air and a slight haze drifts along the horizon in the same general direction as the impressions of tire tracks. Tusk glances over his shoulder, sniffs the breeze, then veers from the path, leading the group on to higher ground.

On a fragmented ridge trail, Tusk maneuvers along the mountainous terrain through the rocks and scrubby trees with Roosevelt and the crew following behind. He stops near an overlooking perch, drops his pack from his shoulder and motions for everyone to stay low and out of sight. In the canyon below, a grouping of men is loosely gathered around the pilfered jeep, safari trucks and supplies.

The native crewmen watch over their cast-off backpacks and hang back as Mogambo and Roosevelt ease themselves along the rocky ledge next to Tusk. They all silently study the layout of the encampment below while making a mental count of the raider's numbers. Roosevelt keeps her head low and whispers.

"Who are those guys?"

On his belly, Tusk holds his rifle at his side and tilts his head and gestures in an unspoken command toward Mogambo. The trusted African scout nods affirmative and moves back to speak with the crewmen. Tusk skootches along the ledge on his chest next to Roosevelt and speaks quietly.

"We know 'em as Diggers ... as in Grave Digger, well-armed mercenaries, probably Somali or other parts of the warring northern regions."

"Cute. What do they want with our gear?"

"They steal supplies and poach ivory to fund their rebellion."

The lady doctor looks down on the group of raiders and watches them move around the partially unloaded trucks.

"Which side are they on?"

"Nobody knows anymore. Guns and money translate to more power."

Tusk points toward the back section of the camp where several pieces of Roosevelt's equipment lay spread out.

"Appears they haven't destroyed your gear yet but they know it's a weapon of some sort."

"I'm guessing there aren't a lot of high-tech computer programmers or drone pilots down there?"

Africa Tusk

The mention of her computer skills casts a worried look over the safari hunter's features. He watches silently a moment and looks over at her with growing concern.

"I shouldn't have brought you."

"Not that again."

Tusk shakes his head and eases further behind the concealing rocks high above the camp.

"If they get their hands on you, then they'll have what's needed to operate that thing. Those men down there are not well-educated, but they can be taught."

"I'd like to say I wouldn't talk, but you'll tell me some gruesome story about how they can make me."

"Right ... we're gonna wait awhile and watch their activity. When it's time, I want you to stay here with Mogambo while I go down there with the drivers."

"What are you planning to do?"

Tusk sits up and puts his hat on. He tugs the wide front brim down as he stares over the ledge into the camp.

"Get my trucks back."

"Don't forget all of my expensive equipment."

The white hunter shoots her an annoyed glance and scoots back away from the rocky ledge.

The morning hours wear along toward noon on the high perch of rocks above the camp. Roosevelt waits and listens as Tusk confers with his crewmen, secluded from the sights and sounds of the raiders in the canyon below. The group falls momentarily silent and Tusk sits quiet while staring at the long wispy clouds passing along the midday horizon.

The warm humid air is stirred by a slight wind and Tusk shifts his position to look over at Roosevelt then Mogambo, waiting patiently in the shade.

"We need to get those men out of the camp."
His eyes settle on Mogambo and their gaze connects as Tusk continues to think aloud.

"What would it take to call those men away?"
The sharp snap of a twig catches their attention and Roosevelt tosses away the stick she was fiddling with. She wipes her hands on her pants leg as she speaks.

"Are we going to sit around all day until they find more elephants to kill?"

The mention of more elephants sparks an idea for both the hunter and gun bearer. Tusk turns to Roosevelt and nods his head with enthusiasm.

"They must have communications with spotters nearby. We get one of those radios and we can give a false lead … a big one that will be too good to let pass."

"Won't they take your trucks with?"

"They won't if they're not working."
Roosevelt wrinkles her forehead, unimpressed.

"I thought you tried that trick before?"

Tusk ignores the lady doctor's mention of the recent blunder with the vehicles and turns to Mogambo. A fleeting shadow passes over as a pair of large carrion birds circle on a rising thermal. Tusk gazes up at them momentarily then speaks in a specific Bantu dialect to Mogambo. Roosevelt listens attentive as the gun bearer merely responds with a silent nod of assent.

Moving from the shade, Mogambo rises to his feet and takes up the double rifle rescued from the raid.

Africa Tusk

The lean figure walks away and disappears silently into the low trees and brush. His soundless exit unsettles Roosevelt as she whispers to Tusk.

"That wasn't Swahili you spoke?"

"No."

"What did you tell him?"

Tusk looks to his crewmen and watches them pass a lit cigarette between themselves.

"I asked him if he could temporarily immobilize our vehicles and get us one of their radios."

"That's kind of dangerous isn't it?"

"Nearly everything about Africa is dangerous. That's why I *asked* him ... not told him."

She peers off into the bush where the loyal safari scout made his exit without a hint of complaint or rebuttal. The crewmen finish their smoke and sit quietly next to the pile of backpacks, staring aloof. The midday heat bears down while Tusk resumes his squatted pose of contemplation, his rifle rested crosswise on his lap.

The canyon below begins to fill with afternoon shadows from the rocks above. The sun's position in the sky transitions toward evening as Tusk and Roosevelt watch the camp's occupants drink and carouse at their leisure. There is no signal of disturbance or any telltale sign of Mogambo's lingering presence. Roosevelt lays her chin on the back of her hand resting on the rocky ledge and looks over at Tusk with the binoculars.

"Do you see him?"

"No ... and you probably won't."

They both remain watchful as the sun sinks lower on the horizon and several campfires are started below. Her observant gaze wanders over to study Tusk who continues studying the camp. She looks to the long barreled rifle constantly at his side and whispers.

"How did you get across that river?"

The binoculars to his face, Tusk's unremitting stare stays on the camp.

"I used the bridge, same as you."

"Did the crocodiles pass?"

Tusk lowers the distance glasses and takes a breath.

"No."

She watches him for any hint of emotion.

"How did you get all wet?"

"I might have slipped on the riverbank."

"You should have crossed when you had Mogambo to spot for you with the rifle?"

The safari hunter grunts and peers over the top of the distance glasses.

"It was getting dark and a shot could be missed. Besides, I didn't want you to see me cry from fear."

Tusk turns his chin slightly and smiles at her. She shakes her head and her eyes dance flirtatiously.

"I doubt that."

"You'll never know."

He faces forward and continues to watch and listen to the activity of the camp down below. Roosevelt eases in closer to his side at the nearing of nightfall and whispers again over his shoulder.

"What's your big plan now?"

Africa Tusk

"If we can lure a lot of those men out of there, we can steal the gear and trucks back before they return."

A humid coolness of evening comes with the breeze as Roosevelt watches the occupants of the secluded valley.

"Will you kill any of them?"

The faint, muted sounds of thumping music and broken laughter carries through the air as the beacons of firelight flash in the fading light of day. Tusk stares intently down at the raider's camp. His features turn dark and heavy as he raises the binoculars again.

"Just as many as I can."

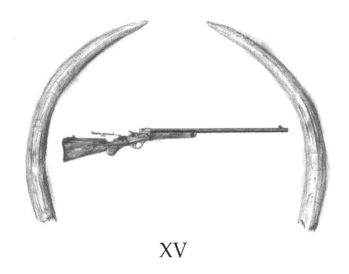

XV

The small safari crew sits quiet, accompanied by the lady doctor in the evening shadows as dusk starts to consume the late afternoon sky. Mogambo returns to the dark camp with barely a sound of breath and flashes a white smile toward Roosevelt before passing Tusk a compact portable radio transmitter. Peering down at the wireless in the near darkness, Tusk stands and addresses his loyal scout.

"Did you take care of the trucks?"
The whites of the dark-skinned man's eyes blink in the low light as Mogambo speaks.

"Easy fix for me 'nd you, Bwana ... not for 'em."

The safari hunter reaches out and rests his free hand on the arm of his longtime friend. Mogambo pushes his chest out with earned pride and Tusk pats the native gun bearer's shoulder with approval.

Africa Tusk

"We'll send the message at first light. I want you to start traveling east with her as soon as we send it." Mogambo nods and moves over toward the others. In the evening shadows, Tusk turns to Roosevelt and can make out her obvious displeasure but interrupts her before she can speak.

"No arguments on this one, please."

Roosevelt stares at Tusk in the dusky light and chews her lip in thought, before uttering her response.

"Just be sure to get all of my equipment."

"It will come out all together or not at all." She shakes her head, pulls her hair back from her neck and blinks her eyes pleadingly at Tusk.

"I can make it worthwhile for you to save it."

"I'll try, but no promises." The lady doctor stands next to Tusk and whispers just loud enough for him to hear.

"Our lives along with those of many animals ... elephants among them, may depend on it."

The two are quiet a moment as the haunting echo of faraway laughter and music travels through the cooling night air from the camp below. Tusk scoots his rifle aside and scrunches down to get in a position of rest on the uneven rocky ground. He crosses his arms across his chest and peers out from under his hat at the doctor.

"Get some sleep while you can. Everything is going to start happening fast just before dawn."

Roosevelt casts her eyes down and looks away before settling in next to her backpack on the ground. Situating the brim of his hat just over his brow, Tusk stares out to the last hint of light on the western horizon.

He settles the felt brim over his face and listens to the muted music from the jam-box floating on the breeze up from the raider camp.

Wakeful hours later, in the chill of pre-dawn, the purple hues of daybreak begin to transform the night sky along the distant hills. Tusk crouches low with his two crewmen squatted nearby with assembled backpacks of gear. He glances over toward Mogambo and Roosevelt as they prepare for the return journey. Clicking the stolen radio several times, he takes a deep breath and speaks in a broken African dialect.

The group sits and waits until there is a reply on the radio and Tusk repeats his message of an elephant herd with several interrupting disconnects from the communicator button. He waits a moment, clicks the receiver several more times and switches the radio volume low before hooking it to his belt. The sky begins to glow brighter with the morning light and Tusk looks up at his small crew and addresses Mogambo.

"Hopefully, that should draw most of them out. Get her moving homebound. We should be able to pick you up across the river."

"Yes, Bwana ... after the river."

Mogambo waits as Roosevelt exchanges an uncertain look of farewell with the white hunter. Tusk nods aware of her mounting concerns and watches the doctor turn to follow her protective chaperon. With a silent gesture, Tusk ushers along the two pack-carrying drivers to follow as he descends a narrow game path down the rocky slope toward the rousing camp below.

Africa Tusk

A truck roars out of camp loaded with men holding automatic rifles. After failed attempts at the ignition of the newly hijacked vehicles, the armed raiders quickly move on to other means of transportation. Concealed in the brush at the edge of camp, Tusk and his men wait for the departing commotion of the poaching expedition to settle.

They wait and watch as the dust haze drifts away leaving the camp setup mostly empty. Tusk's two safari trucks sit parked near the jeep and a pile of supplies along with one other decommissioned vehicle. Under his breath, Tusk mutters to himself.

"Good thought, Mogambo ... an extra vehicle may throw off a bit of suspicion."

Tusk and his retrieval crew, hidden in the bush, watch for any guards posted throughout the camp. The sound of trudging feet catches their attention and they wait as a lone hungover figure wanders between tents. The man carelessly drags his rifle behind, weaving a line in the trampled grass and dirt until he bows low into another canvas dwelling.

In a hushed whisper, Tusk instructs the two crewmen on their recovery plan. He directs each man to a position and motions to the stack of techno-gear that sits piled alongside one of the tarped supply trucks. The three slip from the brush in the early light of morning and stealthily move to the immobilized transportation. Tusk unshoulders his pack, tosses it to the passenger side floor of the jeep and rolls under the front midsection of the deactivated vehicle.

As Tusk and his men work at repairing the sabotaged transportation, a bare-footed mercenary walks near with his machine gun slung over his shoulder. He puts a hip to one of the truck's wheel wells and lights up a homemade cigarette. He puffs, holds the inhale then blows the cloud of smoke overhead.

The large encampment is mostly tranquil with the exception of the muffled jam-box still pumping out a thumping beat. The idle man with the hand-rolled joint slides down to the truck's running board and a waft of skunky-weed smoke drifts down around his ankles. The repairing safari driver positioned under the truck's front axle holds unmoving and waits to resume the fix job. He scrunches his nose and blinks away as the musty stank of ganja drifts by.

The creaking groan of the safari truck's tailgate catches the smoking man's attention and he grabs up his auto rifle to move toward the back of the vehicle. As the armed mercenary slowly steps around the truck's rear panel, Tusk's hard fist slams into his face. The loosely wrapped cigarette explodes against the man's teeth with a burst of sparks and exhaled smoke.

Tusk grabs hold of the machine gun before it hits the ground and the attacked man staggers back a short step before collapsing in a semi-conscious heap. Two motor-grease stained hands reach out from the truck's undercarriage and quickly take hold of the fallen man, dragging him under the vehicle. A sharp steel blade flashes in the shadows beneath the truck and the smoker is nearly beheaded in one deft swipe at the neck.

Africa Tusk

Tusk smooths the sole of his boot over the dusty drag marks on the ground and kicks a clump of loose grass over the dark pool of forming blood. He looks to his other crewman who is now repairing under the jeep and gives an affirming nod. After a searching glance all around, he begins the task of reloading Roosevelt's equipment into the back of the safari trucks.

The raider's camp appears strangely idle with the exception of the beatbox continuously thumping from inside one of the tents. Morning has broken and Tusk stands in the early light with his long-barreled rifle at the ready. He watches his men load the last of the pillaged gear and scans around for any sort of camp activity.

The two safari drivers offer a confirmatory salute and climb into the cabs of the loaded trucks. Tusk returns the gesture with a circular wave of his arm and the trucks roar to life after a hesitant crank of diesel ignitors. A hand gripped at the side of the flipped down windscreen, Tusk hops into the Willys Jeep and cranks the key. The post-war, vintage jeep fires up instantly and he pounds his foot on the clutch as he smacks the shifter into gear.

Tusk raises his arm high, points forward and hollers to his crew in the broken silence, above the clamor of the various engines.

"Move 'em out boys!"

The supply trucks grind into gear and Tusk leans his gun over the dashboard along the folded flat windscreen. He directs the single shot rifle's aim around the camp as the two trucks jerk forward and roll slowly past the jeep.

The canvas tent flap at the source of the unpleasant music flutters with movement and Tusk refocuses his attention.

A shirtless man bursts from the dwelling with an auto rifle in hand and raises the weapon toward the rolling trucks. Tusk squeezes the trigger on his long-gun and the man spins to the ground, throwing the firearm aside. Quickly reloading the single shot hunting rifle, Tusk ducks down as a gun muzzle pokes from another tent and rips off several rounds of semi-auto gunfire.

From the cutaway jeep side, rifle tucked at his shoulder, the experienced marksmen sends a shot into the forward stock of the automatic weapon, taking it out of commission. The damaged weapon drops to the dirt and a howl of inflicted pain rises up from inside the tent where the concealed figure hides. Tusk draws his .45 sidearm and snaps several shots into the smoky canvas dwelling. The attacker slumps under the flap door as Tusk releases pressure from the clutch and jams his foot on the gas pedal.

The jeep's rear wheels spin and fishtail on the dry terrain sending a plume of dirt over the decapitation casualty left behind. Another man dashes from inside a tent and Tusk lays down pistol fire causing the man to dive away. He steers the jeep into the camp, through the cloudy haze created by the escaping supply trucks.

Several shots whiz alongside, plinking into the bush as Tusk drives toward the far side of the poacher encampment. He spots a pile of recently harvested elephant ivory stacked next to several fuel supply containers and aims his cocked pistol over his driving arm.

Africa Tusk

The pistol kicks back and Tusk hammers on the trigger until the automatic slide jacks to an empty receiver.

Subsequent sparks off metal fuel canisters, a delayed explosion rocks the ground. The heat of the blast topples nearby tents in a wave of fiery inferno. Flaming brush and canvas quickly extents across the camp, punctuated by muffled eruptions of kerosene lamps. Ducking low to avoid airborne shrapnel, Tusk shifts up through the gears and careens the jeep away from the exploding blaze of fire that consumes the ill-gotten elephant ivory.

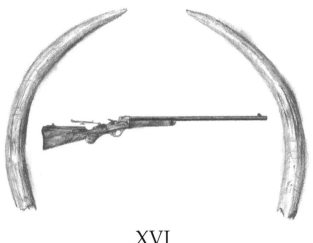

XVI

A hustle of small female safari boots follows close to the set of long, dark sandaled feet. Roosevelt looks behind as a rising cloud of black smoke and bursting fire erupts from the mercenary camp. Mogambo takes a quick glance over his shoulder and urges her to continue along at a quickened pace.

"We make distance, Memsahib. Them's coming." With a shortness of breath, Roosevelt mutters aloud.

"Something like that could be spotted for miles."

"Bwana Tusk ... he not do things small."

Mogambo starts into a loping pace and Roosevelt quickly follows at his long-striding, leather strapped heels. They promptly traverse a field of grazed down brush and slide into a wide thicket of head-high elephant grass. Maneuvering along a narrow herd trail, the long sprouts of greenery rise up and arch over their path.

Africa Tusk

Finally clear of the tall grasses, the route ahead contains thickets of stout thorny trees along their course. They continue at a hurried pace with Roosevelt sweating through her torn blouse and Mogambo glistening like fresh asphalt. They crest a small hill and pushing their way through clinging brambles until they break into another clearing.

Out in the open they are surprised to be greeted by a group of several military looking trucks. The mercenary looking troops assembled across their path of travel all have guns out and ready for action. Mogambo hurries to unsling the double rifle from his shoulder and steps in front of Roosevelt protectively.

A second rush of armed men emerges from the thick surrounding cover and surrounds their position. Mogambo tucks the rifle stock to his shoulder, snaps off the safety and prepares to make a desperate stand of ground. He whispers over his shoulder to Roosevelt.

"I shoot, you run."

The chattering of various African dialects comes from every direction as Roosevelt looks over the dire situation and prepares to flee. Several men circle around with rifles raised and toothy grins coming from dark, tattooed features. She places her hand on Mogambo's shoulder and speaks with bold composure.

"Put down the gun, let's not end it here."

His eyes dart back at her and he shakes his head.

"We may no get another chance, Memsahib."

"This isn't much of an option."

Roosevelt looks to the waiting trucks and then around at the dozen vicious raiders prepared to execute them with little regard. Everyone stares blankly toward her and the chattering of voices ceases. A seemingly long time passes before Roosevelt finally raises her hands and speaks out.

"I will not resist you ... we surrender."

Mogambo drops his gaze and reluctantly lowers the rifle. The mercenary figures are quickly upon the protective gun bearer and he is disarmed and pushed to the ground. Separating the captives, Mogambo is pummeled with repeated punches and kicks from booted feet. Roosevelt tries to lunge forward to protect him but is restrained by a tight hold on her arms.

A stinging pain encircles her wrists as they are hastily lashed behind her back with plastic zip-ties. She starts to call out and is quickly muted by a firm set of clenched knuckles that smashes her head above the ear and jolts her head violently. A wave of pain and anguish sweeps through her being as the light of day blurs then fades to unconsciousness.

A convoy of camouflage-painted trucks rumbles and bounds across remote African territory. Several lean whipcord looking mercenaries stand along running-boards with a firm grip on the vehicle while holding government surplus automatic rifles. The last truck in the transport is a military troop hauler with black canvas tarpon covering the cargo area. The rolled up sides allow for air circulation but provide little relief from the heat for the occupants inside.

Africa Tusk

Sweat streams down Roosevelt's temples as she sits bound and tied with her back against the forward portion of the cargo bed. On the floorboards surrounded by booted feet is the unconscious form of Mogambo who bounces freely with the bumpy movements of the truck. Roosevelt looks up to the hollow, dark faces of their captors and can see the obvious disregard for human life in their rebellion-hardened eyes.

Two parked safari trucks and a Willys Jeep wait alongside the edge of the meandering river. Standing inside the jeep with one boot rested on the passenger seat, Tusk scans the empty expanse all around with his binoculars. A grunt of frustration escapes his lips as he lowers the distance glasses and sinks down into the thinly padded seat of the vehicle.

"Mogambo should have been here by now."
He looks at his wristwatch then over his shoulder at the two waiting trucks and curses under his breath.
"Damn women ..."

The peak temps of afternoon have passed and the jeep's wheels remain parked at the water's edge. The mud-tinged river rushes behind, teeming with various sorts of wildlife. Tusk stands on the gravel shore with his long-gun in hand waiting for the now unlikely rendezvous with Mogambo and Roosevelt. He turns to watch downriver as the safari trucks transverse the shallow crossing, pushing water aside as they steer toward the opposite bank.

The engines choke and cough as they heave the sturdy vehicles onto the gravely bank, dripping water from the doors and undercarriage. The drivers give a brief waving salute out the windows as they feather the throttles to clear water from the diesel engines then continue traveling away to the east.

He watches the vehicles disappear over the far rise of hills and listens as the motor noise fades into the distance. Tusk turns to his jeep, stands thinking a moment and shakes his head in doubt. He takes a few steps closer to the lone vehicle and sighs.

"I can't believe I'm doing this ..."

The roofless jeep is overladen with hard cases and bundles of Roosevelt's experimental gear. Mounted in the back between the narrow jump seats is the anti-poaching weapon accompanied by the flying drone and support equipment. The jeep appears to be a post war surplus vehicle fixed with space-aged technology linked to some sort of futuristic cannon.

Tusk heaves a booted foot through the side door cutout and slides into the driver's seat. He looks to the laptop computer perched auspiciously on the passenger seat and groans to himself.

"If she doesn't turn up quick, I'll have second thoughts 'nd dump this whole load of crap in the river."

The irritated safari hunter fires up the jeep, jams it into gear and tears off in a whirl of spinning wheels away from the meandering waterway. The late afternoon sun blazes brightly as the bizarrely loaded vehicle silhouette heads in a westerly direction, returning along the previously traveled path.

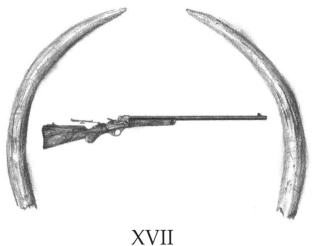

XVII

The sounds of wildlife from the African night swell in the air as the military trucks rumble along and begin to slow. Surrounded by mud-caked, dusted over military boots while restrained on the floorboards, Roosevelt looks out past the seated bodies to glimpse lighted torches and thatched roof dwellings. The transport vehicles roll through the native village and she notices the expression of her captor's features transition from idle boredom to the excitement of homecoming.

Roosevelt's backside slams into the cargo bed as the truck jolts to a halt and the excited men leap over the sides with rifles casually in hand. The tailgate drops and Mogambo's unconscious form is dragged from the truck bed and tossed to the ground. Roosevelt stares into the dark sky contrasted against the glaring flames of light as two men reach in and pull at her booted feet.

She kicks out at their gasping reach and laughter erupts from the assembled men. Several more hands reach in and she is quickly pulled from the cargo area and put on her feet in front of a large crowd of innocent looking villagers. The children, dressed in dirty yet colorful shorts and shirts, smile openly at her as she is led through the crowd by the hardened mercenaries.

The wide-eyes surrounding Roosevelt marvel at her light color hair and stab out from the crowd with a desire to have a fleeting touch of her ivory skin. Her handlers shove the gathered crowd aside and Roosevelt is pushed into a large thatch and beam hut. The interior is sparsely lit by candles and oil lamps which cause her to squint as she is ushered forward.

Roosevelt gazes at the elaborately furnished, primitive dwelling and observes a suited, well-groomed Asian gentleman sitting behind a carved wooden desk. Of Chinese decent, Su Long Hang appears to be middle-aged with thin streaks of graying along his black, slicked-back hair. His lowered features, obscured in shadow, have the iniquitous presence of a tax assessor or dour government agent.

Hang looks up slightly and rises from his desk chair. His countenance remains unemotional as he astutely studies the tall womanly form of the doctor before him. The dark pupils of his slanted eyes upon her, Roosevelt stands uncomfortable in his gaze. She flexes her hands under the plastic ties around her wrists and stands rigid as she speaks.

"Who are you?"

Africa Tusk

The room is silent and the crackle of the flame in the lanterns is almost discernable above the din of crowd noise outside. Roosevelt turns to the guards blocking the doorway then back toward the desk.

"And where is my friend?"

Hang nods and gestures to the men at the door. There is a slight murmur between the two mercenaries, then one of them steps outside.

The dimly-lit office is quiet as Hang stands behind the desk watching Roosevelt. She anxiously waits for what happens next as the door is kicked aside behind her. Turning, she watches as the limp, bound form of Mogambo is unceremoniously dragged across the threshold and dumped on the floor.

Roosevelt stares at her native protector a moment until she notices him catch a shallow lungful of breath. She turns back to Hang as he steps around to the side of the elaborately carved writing desk. The small statured gentleman nods his chin toward the newly arrived captive on the floor.

"Are you satisfied now?"

"Hardly."

The Asian man stands uncomfortably straight with his shoulders pulled back as he moves around to the front of the desk. His dark eyes blink as he continues the assessment of the female figure before him.

"I was expecting something more ..."

She interrupts him and sneers under his gaze.

"Scientific?"

Hang shifts his stern demeanor and forces a smile.

"There you are ... that is the word."

The amicable grin quickly fades and the Asian man's features become slightly grim.

"Why are you here?"

"Your army of goons brought me here."

With a compulsory grunt, Hang clears his throat and steps back to lean his hands behind on the desktop.

"No. Why are you in Africa?"

Roosevelt takes a deep chest-full of air, feigns confidence and tries to distract her mind from the throbbing pain of the plastic binding around her wrists.

"I'm a Doctor."

"Oh, really? What kind is that?"

"I'm here to help animals."

Hang shakes his head skeptically and his dark beady eyes pierce right through her.

"Stop the lies. We already know you are not a traditional practitioner. We have good information that you are from one of those Animal Rights Institutes."

Roosevelt stands in the center of the room and glares at Hang as he continues his detailed assessment of her.

"You are a specialist of the ivory trade. You arrived on the continent five days ago, met with your government contact and were escorted to a safari service before traveling to the interior."

"Why are you asking questions if you already know everything about me?

"A mere courtesy."

"Do you plan to kill me?"

The Chinese businessman watches her carefully.

"I am against violence myself."

Africa Tusk

Roosevelt gives an obvious look behind at the armed men guarding the door, backed by several more outside.

Su Long Hang nods slowly and crosses his sleeve-shirted arms across his narrow chest.

"Violence is bad for business … and I'm here in Africa running a business."
The thoughts of murdered elephants begin to well up anger in Roosevelt as she speaks through clenched teeth.

"A business in poached ivory?"

"No. I enable the harvesting of what Africa has provided for its native peoples. You are a foreigner and would not understand the economic forces at play or societal dynamics of cropping."
On the floor Mogambo makes a groaning sound and shifts slightly as he gets a lungful of air. Roosevelt looks down at him then up at Su Long Hang.

"You look a long way from home yourself."

"My family has done business dealings on this continent for centuries. I bring wealth and prosperity."

She looks around at the exotic carved furnishings then to the woven walls of the indigenous hut.

"Your lush accommodations really show it."
Hang glares at her, not enjoying her derogatory sarcasm.

"For someone in your uncertain situation, your tongue should be less sharp."

"What situation is that exactly?"
Hang bobs his head for calculated effect with his words.

"You are an uninvited visitor who has gone missing in a hostile land filled with unsavory characters. Instead of insulting your host, you should be wondering what we plan to do with you."

"The question has crossed my mind."

Hang uncrosses his arms, rubs his hands together and places his palms again on the desktop.

"When I sent my men to fetch the new arrival and they only obtained your equipment and gear, I saw it as a rare opportunity."

Su Long Hang stands up straight, pauses then walks over to Roosevelt. He circles her slowly with a measured pace and glances down at Mogambo still unconscious on the floor. The distinct swishing click of a switchblade knife perks Roosevelt's senses and she feels the plastic binding at her wrists release tension with a swipe of the razor-sharp device. As the foreign capitalist continues around behind his female captive, he speaks at a low hissing whisper from one ear to the next.

"We have for a longtime known the famed reputation of the white hunter called Tusk. When we heard communications that you had enlisted his services for a jaunt into our vicinity, we saw the occasion to let's say ... kill two birds with one stone."

Hang steps closer and places his small hand on the nape of her neck. The clammy touch of the poaching kingpin sends cold chills down her spine. Roosevelt shrugs off his grip and looks over her shoulder at his small stature backlit by a kerosene lantern behind.

"Well, only half your plan worked. Tusk and his crew are long gone by now."

"Not true. He will be here shortly... I'm almost sure of it."

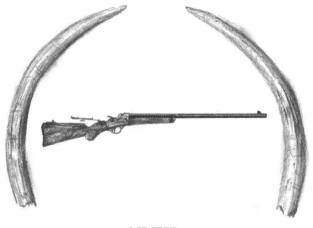

XVIII

The Willys Jeep rolls to a stop in the cool haze of daybreak. Tusk swings a leg over the side, slides out and kneels down to study the mix of tread markings along the ground. He paces the area counting the tire and boot imprints all around. The morning sun begins to rise over the hills on the horizon and Tusk turns to stare off in the opposite direction.

"Damn, the same trucks I chased out yesterday."

Tusk hoists himself back into the seat behind the steering wheel and stabs his foot on the clutch pedal, pushing it to the floorboard. He revs the engine and eases the shifter into low gear. Staring toward the distinctive tire tracks in the early light, Tusk shakes his head uncertain, hammers on the gas and roars off along the trail to the west.

Inside another thatched hut, devoid of any luxury furnishings or windows, Roosevelt sits in a corner and watches Mogambo on the floor slowly returning to consciousness. She crawls over to his side and supports his head in her lap.

"Easy there Mogambo, take it slow."

Mogambo relaxes his body and peers up at her with his gleaming white eyes and whispers faintly.

"Is anyone watching?"

She stares down at him with surprise and carefully looks around the empty windowless hut.

"No, I don't think so."

Flashing a grin, Mogambo lies comfortable in the doctor's cradling arms and winks at her.

"We need to get out of here, Memsahib."

Roosevelt looks to the door and the faint light of a new day creeps through the cracks from outside.

"Do you even know where we are?"

"When you say we not fight, figure a knock on head is best to last the duration."

Astounded, Roosevelt sighs in relief and realizes that Mogambo hasn't been injured too severely after all.

"You've been listening all this time?"

"I took small sleep for a bit."

"How badly are you hurt?"

The native safari guide touches a swelled lump on his skull where they whacked him with the rifle stock.

"It hurt, yes, but dead hurt much, much worse."

Roosevelt softly laughs at her native companion's seeming attempt at humor. She peers down at the prone form of Mogambo and whispers.

"Well, if you're dead it shouldn't hurt too badly." Mogambo looks up at her with a straight face and utters.

"I have friends and family it would hurt plenty."

The hostage doctor takes a moment to reflect on his keen perspective and gazes around cautiously. A gentle breeze flutters the door of the hut and she looks down at Mogambo.

"How will we get out of this village?"

"You kept alive for value. Mine not worthwhile." Roosevelt nods.

"Then you need to escape."

"Yes, but won't be far."

There is a sound of heavy booted footfalls by the threshold and Mogambo's eyes quickly shut, his body falling limp. Roosevelt stares down at the gun bearer then hears the door to the thatched dwelling open. A narrow shaft of sunlight from outside moves across the dirt floor until Roosevelt and Mogambo are in its lighted path. She squints to the broad, backlighted form in the doorway and to the early sky of morning beginning to brighten into day.

Jacket-sleeves rolled back on muscled forearms, a deeply tanned, White Hunter enters and steps aside from the sunlit threshold. Roosevelt lets her eyes adjust and observes that the figure is dressed in similar safari gear as others she has witnessed but has a hulking menace to his presence. This particular professional hunter is widely known around Africa as a gun-for-hire and opportunist with unpopular opinions about exotic game being merely, cash on the hoof, ripe for harvest.

He moves toward Roosevelt and peers past her shoulder at Mogambo, laid out on the floor. A hint of recognition flashes in his piercing eyes and a knowing smile appears on chiseled, windswept features.

"Is he still alive?"

Roosevelt glances up at the looming figure.

"Barely. He's still unconscious."

A pained yelp emits from the female doctor as the man roughly grabs her by the hair and pulls her up and away.

Mogambo's head drops limply to the dirt floor, lying motionless at an awkward slant. Roosevelt gasps with discomfort as the cruel man continues to hold her by the scalp. He directs her across the dirt floor and shoves Roosevelt aside with a grunt.

"We'll see, won't we?"

The man delivers a wide sweeping kick to the prone man's midsection that sounds painfully well-connected. A rush of air blows out from the body as Mogambo lifts into the air and slams violently into the thatched wall, unresponsive. Roosevelt rushes ahead and tries to maneuver around the forceful assailant.

"What kind of animal are you?"

Satisfied with Mogambo's unconscious condition, the man turns his attention back to Roosevelt as the daylight glints across his hard demeanor.

"I'm practiced hereabouts and I know all the tricks of these natives. Peter Logan, at yer service."

He bends at the waist with a sarcastic flourish and takes a firm hold of her upper arm. Through her cotton sleeve, the strength of his vice-like grip squeezes to the bone.

Africa Tusk

She grits her teeth and hisses at him as the clutching force sends a throbbing pain through her being.

"Let go of me you … you brute!"

"Brute, eh? 'Fraid not, Missy. The Chinaman wants to see you again and he's not to be disappointed."

At the edge of the African village, concealed in the low hanging trees and underbrush, a brief reflected glimmer reveals a sheltered position in the scrub. Tusk attentively watches the activity of the settlement through his field glasses. He makes a mental count of trucks, armed mercenaries and seemingly blameless bystanders.

After studying the occupants of the village for a time, the secluded hunter picks up his long gun and stealthily maneuvers the barrel through the surrounding thicket of brush. He tucks the wooden stock to his shoulder, clicks back the hammer and raises the rifle to his cheek. Tusk lines up his range-adjusted sights on one of the unsuspecting, armed mercenaries who stands smoking next to a military style truck. He takes a sedative breath, holds steady and wraps his forefinger around the readied trigger.

Suddenly his ears perk to the faint sound of a small twig breaking not far behind on his flank. Tusk hesitantly lowers the gun from his cheek and readies to turn in defense when a dark, sleek figure slides in alongside through the bush. The smooth calming voice of Mogambo whispers through the leafy foliage as Tusk instantly recognizes his missing companion.

"Just like old times, eh Bwana?"

In a series of descending clicks, Tusk thumbs the rifle's hammer down and removes his finger from the trigger. Relieved, he turns to face the unassuming smile of Mogambo and attempts to conceal his concern when he looks to the swollen mound on his friend's temple.

"You okay? Where's the girl?"

"Small hut … just south of largest one."

Tusk looks to the lodging arrangement in the village and speaks low as he raises the binoculars with his off hand.

"I told you to watch over her."

"Better from out here, than dead."

Tusk nods amenable and lowers the eyepieces.

"Who's running the show in there?"

"Chinese businessman gives orders. Thirty or more Diggers with guns … and Logan on hire."

"Damn, Logan is down there?"

The rifle is set aside and Tusk picks up his field glasses again. He peers through the circular lenses, adjusts the focus ring and murmurs.

"That's a big operation."

Mogambo squats alongside Tusk in the concealing brush and holds his knees to his chest.

"They get message about large herd of Tuskers. Deciding now to harvest ivory or set trap for you."

"They know I'm coming?"

Mogambo stares ahead into the poacher camp and nods affirmative as Tusk studies the setup through the long distance glasses then slowly lowers them.

"Well, let's not disappoint them."

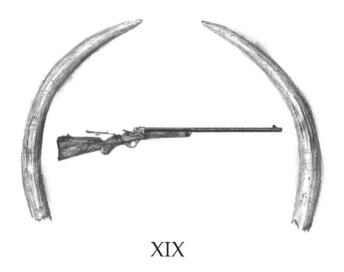

XIX

There is a hurried surge of general activity in the village as trucks are driven around and loaded with automatic rifles, boxes of ammunition, fuel canisters and chainsaws. Logan barks exacting commands as he walks among the common village dwellers and harvesting crew while checking provisions. A native tribesman stops before him, gives a military salute and utters a short burst of information in the local dialect.

With a nod, Logan dismisses the man and looks toward the largest thatch lodge near the center of the village. A strange feeling of being watched comes over him as his gaze continues to travel around the perimeter of the village. He pauses to let the paranoid sensation pass and takes one more survey of the mercenary crew before striding away to meet with the Chinaman.

Inside the large thatched structure, Roosevelt sits in a chair opposite Su Long Hang. He bends over the map on his desk and he traces a finger along the detailed geography of the terrain. He murmurs several words to himself in Chinese then peeks mischievously up at her and flicks his tongue against the inner side of his teeth.

"Decisions, decisions ..."

Hang stands to his full five foot stature and leans forward with his palms on the desktop.

"There is a large herd of Tuskers moving just a few hours from here and I don't think we have time to play 'bait and wait' for your knight in brown khaki."

Roosevelt stares ahead at him with disgust.

"You're a sick man."

Hang lets a hinting smile tickle the edges of his thin lips.

"I'm a rich man and if I want to remain that way, I need to harvest this herd. Your pal, the legendary 'Tusk' will have to wait for another time."

The Chinese businessman grunts with amusement, takes a cigarette from a carved ivory tray on the desk, lights up and offers one to Roosevelt who declines.

The burning Asian tobacco mixes with the damp smell of thatch, prominent in the air from the morning mist. Hang takes a long drag on the rolled smoke and resumes his study of the map. Pushing the chair back and rising to her feet, Roosevelt stands before Su Long Hang to display her best assets. She tries to engage his primal interest with carnal diplomacy in a dire attempt at saving the targeted elephant herd.

"How far away are they?"

Africa Tusk

Hang glances up from the map on the desktop and her physical topography does not go unnoticed by the mature gentleman. He speaks slowly, distracted as his gaze takes in her womanly curves.

"A few hours possibly ... depending on the water supply and terrain."

"Seems like a long way to go."

"In Shanghi, it may take several hours to get across town but that is the price of business.

"What if the herd isn't really there?"

Su Long Hang smiles as he takes another long drag from the cigarette then exhales.

"You think a trick perhaps?"

"A very large herd sounds too good to be true."

The Chinaman behind the desk returns his attention to the map and circles an area before making a note. His eyes slowly rise to address Roosevelt.

"You imagine this might be a false alarm as when we let Mister Kalispell retrieve his vehicles?

A slight tremor of shock races through Roosevelt's being.

"You let him do that?"

"It was rather easy for him, wasn't it?"

"Why?"

"We wanted you and your skills. The trucks had no information or insight into your operation."

Hang stands and places his hands behind his back.

"Yes, of course, they were supposed to kill him and not let them destroy a small stash of ivory, but we'll get him next time."

Su Long Hang steps around from behind the desk and leans on the front edge. He studies the female doctor in front of him as she nervously evaluates her options. Hang lets a wicked grin percolate his features.

"I do have something you may find very interesting Missus Roosevelt ... Hamilton ... Adams."

"You know who I am?"

"We knew most everything about you as soon as you stepped off that plane from your connection with the United Kingdom."

She stares ahead at Su Long Hang with contempt, but remains silent as the slick-haired businessman continues his inquest.

"We have an unfortunate situation for you to answer to. I received news about our new helicopter going down several days ago."

He watches her for any hint of reaction as he continues.

"Mister Tusk and a well-placed shot with that rifle of his could bring down a chopper possibly, but I have reports of a dozen men cut down in mere seconds."

Hang's dark eyes bore into her as his temper steadily rises beneath his seemingly calm demeanor.

"I don't imagine an American Cowboy with a single-shot long gun can shoot that quick or efficiently."

A trickle of nervous sweat glistens down Roosevelt's temple and she breaks her stoic gaze with the probing Chinaman.

"So, Doctor ... you know something about it?"

She turns back at Su Long Hang and maintains her poise.

"I just joined with his safari convoy a few days ago to photograph and survey the health of local herds."

"Interesting? That's exactly when it happened."

Africa Tusk

The haze from the burning cigarette fills the dank air in the lodge as Hang continues his interrogation.

"I had a crew round up your camp supplies and they reported an abundant amount of electronic gear and unusual ammunition. Coincidence, I think not?"

Su Long Hang stares at Roosevelt a long uncomfortable moment and she clenches her jaw tightly to steel her nerve. He stands before the broad carved desk and flashes an evil grin that make his narrow eyes twinkle with malice.

"It's decided then. You will accompany us for the ivory harvest. It is a disagreeable task sometimes, but it pays very well."

The front entrance of the largest lodge swings open and Roosevelt steps out into the daylight. She lets her eyes adjust to the bright rays of sun and is urged forward by an armed guard. The trucks are lined up in the center of the village and Su Long Hang appears from the doorway behind her. They stand and watch as the mercenary army is mobilized for the reaping of ivory.

Approaching from the line of trucks, Peter Logan strolls over to them. He stops before Su Long Hang and turns to give Roosevelt a lecherous gaze.

"Mornin' to you, Madam. Miss me much?"
He looms over the diminutive Chinaman and pulls back his shoulders in a blatant display of manliness.

"You summoned me, Sir?"

Hang steps past Logan and surveys the assemblage of poacher crew and transport vehicles.

"She will join us for our job of work."

In a crude carnal gesture, Logan smiles as he wipes the opening of his mouth with thick calloused fingers.

"I'll clear a place for her to sit."

He gives her a smarmy wink as she tries to suppress a revolting shiver. Logan pivots on his boot heel next to Hang and snorts aloud.

"What about Tusk?"

The lineup of support trucks sit idle and the fumes from the diesel exhaust wafts through the village, causing Roosevelt to feel nauseous. Su Long Hang plunges his small hand deep in his pocket and sniffs deeply the acrid aroma. He glances over at Logan and nods confidently.

"Kill his safari native so there is nothing left for him here in the village. He will have to follow us for the woman and we can lay a trap for him nearer to the site."

Logan shifts his weight in his tall elephant-hide boots and hunches his shoulders submissively.

"Uh, he is gone already."

Hang peers up at the large hunter next to him.

"Gone as in already dead, I presume?"

"No ... he's just gone."

Redness flushes the pale skin of the diminutive man and he glares ahead at the harvesting crew still loading the last remaining supplies. He speaks with his attention forward but directs his harsh words at Logan.

"Your village idiots can't even detain and keep watch over a tied-up, unconscious man!

Without missing a beat, Logan shrugs off his employer's anger.

"Apparently not. Anything else?"

Africa Tusk

A brief sense of relief calms Roosevelt at the news of Mogambo's escape. She feels Logan's eyes upon her but gives his scrutiny a cold reception. Hang notices the hostile energy transpiring between the two and folds his arms across his chest, turning away.

"Have them bring over my personal transport for the lady and myself."

Logan shoots another lecherous look toward Roosevelt.

"She's welcome to ride with me and the boys."

Roosevelt sneers at the mercenary behind Hang's back and the professional hunter enjoys the attention. She takes a step away and spits her words at Logan.

"Sorry to decline your generous invitation Mister Logan. I'll enjoy the thought of you crashing into a deep ravine and getting what you justly deserve."

The mercenary safari hunter chuckles, salutes them and struts away toward the convoy of vehicles. Su Long Hang glances back at Roosevelt and speaks in a low serious tone.

"He has an obvious liking for you, I see. He seems a crude manner of beast for sure, but a necessary evil in the untamed wilds of the African frontier."

Hang stares at Roosevelt until she finally makes eye contact with him. The shimmer in his slanted gaze shows a calculated guile.

"Be careful ... or you will be at his pleasure."

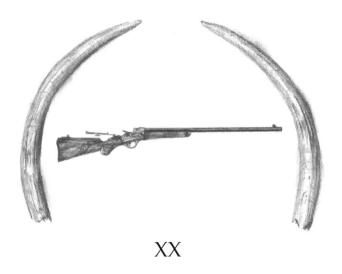

XX

The sun rises in the sky toward mid-morning as the large convoy of mercenary vehicles roars through the village. Just past the last hut on the outskirts of the settlement, the forward truck grinds its breaks to a halt and every truck behind jerks to an unexpected standstill. The black Mercedes G-class, off-road SUV, transporting Su Long Hang and his female guest almost crashes into the vehicle ahead as it skids to a sliding stop.

Inside the dark window tinted vehicle, Hang pushes back from the backrest of the driver before him and recovers from the shock of the sudden jolt. He settles back into the cushion of his own leather seat, visually fuming with annoyance. Roosevelt smiles as she watches the small statured man dig at his feet to pick up the charts and papers that fell from his lap.

"You should be wearing your seatbelt."

Africa Tusk

Hang glances over at Roosevelt, then looks past her out the darkened side window. He ignores her snarky comment and yells to the driver in front of him.

"What the hell? Why are we stopped?"

The driver looks back nervously and stammers in a heavy local accent.

"All the trucks are stopped, Sir."

Su Long Hang looks at Roosevelt suspiciously then reaches into the seat pouch before him and draws out an automatic pistol. Her eyes dart to the seat pouch in front of her and with veiled disappointment, discovers it empty. Hang grumbles as he slides the full clip from the handle of the firearm, inspects it and reinserts it.

"This is likely initiated by your new associate."

A cold shiver of panic sweeps over Roosevelt as she watches Hang chamber a round into the handgun's receiver. He opens his door and peers around the dark window toward the front of the convoy.

"He will almost certainly die today."

Hang steps out of the vehicle and tries to look past the line of trucks as Peter Logan arrives next to him and glances curiously inside at Roosevelt.

"What's going on?"

The Chinese businessman looks down at the hunting rifle in his associate's hands and growls.

"That's your job to know, isn't it?"

The supply trucks ahead all rumble at an idle as Logan tucks the scoped rifle to a ready position at his shoulder. He slowly advances forward with Su Long Hang following at his shirt tails. As they move clear of the open door, Roosevelt slides across the bench seat.

She is about to crawl outside when her planned path of escape slams shut and the door bolt locks into place.

Hang taps the barrel of his handgun on the driver-side window glass and it slowly rolls down. His hushed voice can be heard clearly by the chauffeur along with Roosevelt in the rear passenger seat.

"Keep her in there until we find out what this is. You have my permission to shoot her if you have to."
Su Long Hang's beady eyes peek back at Roosevelt over the driver's shoulder and they twinkle with malice as the dark window slides up and blocks out the light.

At the edge of a scrubby clearing, about fifty meters from the last structure in the village and the halted trucks, a solitary man stands in the dirt track. Logan and Su Long Hang walk up alongside the vehicles and push through the forming crowd of natives. The dark-skinned tribesmen whisper and chatter reverently amongst themselves about who it might be and Hang tilts his head to Logan with the obvious question.

"Who is that?"

Logan lowers the sights of his rifle and eyes the sole occupant in the clearing. Remaining suspicious at all times, he studies the empty void behind all the way back to the near edge of the brush-line.

"That's the one they call *Tusk*."
The Chinaman studies the lone unarmed figure in the path and gives a discontented snort.

"Ahh! I was expecting someone bigger."

Logan glances over at the diminutive stature of Hang and cautiously watches for some sort of ambush.

Africa Tusk

"He's big enough ... and bigger than most."
Hang glares up at Logan and sneers.

"Then what is he doing, just standing there?"
The mercenary gunman stares across the expanse to the professional safari hunter in the trail and shrugs.

"You're the boss-man, go ahead and ask 'em."

The small Chinaman puffs himself up to his full measure and appears confident with the armed support of Logan and the mercenary crew. Out of the trucks the tribesmen all stand with rifles in hand, waiting and watching the unusual encounter. At the forefront, Su Long Hang considers the numbers to his overwhelming advantage and whispers aside to Logan.

"I don't trust whatever this man, Tusk, is doing. If something appears queer, shoot him down like a dog."

Logan nods with agreement and raises the tip of his rifle to put Tusk in the crosshairs of his scope.

"This whole situation is a bit peculiar."

"Well, don't shoot him yet until things progress." Hang lowers his handgun to his side and moves several steps forward. He forces an insincere smile and squints at the solitary man standing in the dusty path.

"So ... you are the mighty 'Tusk'?"

A slight breeze comes from behind as Tusk stands with his arms hanging unthreateningly at his side. His calculating gaze travels across the assembled crowd of mercenary tribesmen and settles on the Asian man advancing toward him. Hang slowly walks closer and tilts his head to question the lone individual.

"Are you alone or is this some sort of an elaborate trap? What are you meaning to accomplish?"

Eric H. Heisner

Tusk waits patient as Hang takes several more steps closer then halts a safe distance away.

"I want to make an exchange for the woman."

Su Long Hang grins at the implied intrigue.

"What have you to offer?"

"The anti-poaching technology is the swap."

The two stand in silence until Hang finally speaks.

"Seems to be a fascinating trade, but wouldn't it be to our advantage to just kill you here and now?"

Tusk glances behind at the distance to the cover of trees and Logan steps up beside Hang and whispers.

"We've got 'em dead to rights. He's trapped and will never make the brush before we cut him down."

Su Long Hang nods and calls out to Tusk.

"Mister Kalispell, you have put yourself in a severely compromised position. You must provide us with this so-called anti-poaching weapon or you will be killed where you stand."

The solitary figure takes a step forward and stands firm.

The native gunmen at the trucks all watch with interest as the famed white hunter closes the distance to their disreputable employer. Tusk speaks in a low voice, just loud enough to be heard the short distance away by Su Long Hang and Logan.

"Then you'll never find it and the trained support team will have it in the field working against you within the week. Your operation will be put out of commission and you'll most likely be captured or killed."

Logan stares ahead, still holding his rifle at the ready and speaks in a hushed tone beside Hang.

"He's only bluffing, there is no such thing."

Africa Tusk

The Asian ivory trader moves forward with Peter Logan following closely at his heels. The opposing parties are now only a few meters apart and Hang reads the passive demeanor of his capable adversary. Modifying his improvised strategy, Hang attempts to counter the engagement with a personal appeal.

"Your contemporary, Mister Logan here believes you are running a bluff. Do you have solid proof of any anti-poaching equipment or the implied ramifications?"

Tusk puts on a forced grin and lets his eyes travel over to Peter Logan with the rifle at his shoulder.

"Come up any short on your headcount lately? A downed helicopter and a dozen men baking in the sun should help you believe me."

Logan lifts his cheek from the gunstock and calls out.

"Was that your doings?"

The amused look falls from Tusk's features and his eyes divert to a dark SUV moving up the column of trucks.

"That was the handiwork of the anti-poaching technology. You release the girl and I'll take you to it."

The Chinese businessman pauses to think a minute while he studies Tusk's shrewd behavior carefully.

"You want me to release her and trust you?"

"That's correct."

"I have a slightly better option."

Tusk's steady gaze moves to Logan then to the numerous automatic weapons pointed at him from the native mercenaries lined up in front of the trucks.

"Yeah … let me guess?"

Su Long Hang flashed an overexcited grin.

"We don't want to shoot you, yet. How about you come along with us on our harvest, then we'll go find that mystery weapon of yours?"

Tusk's eyes dart back to Hang.

"And you let the girl go?"

"No, she will stay with us."

All eyes are upon Tusk as he shakes his head slowly and moves a hand behind his back.

"No deal."

The rattle of auto rifles coming to the ready fills the air until Su Long Hang raises his arm in a halting gesture. Dozens of military surplus firearms are raised and directed at Tusk in a menacing fashion. Logan and the Chinese businessman take several exaggerated steps backward as to not be caught in the impending crossfire and Hang speaks aloud with a clear commanding tone.

"Mister Tusk … I'm afraid, I insist."

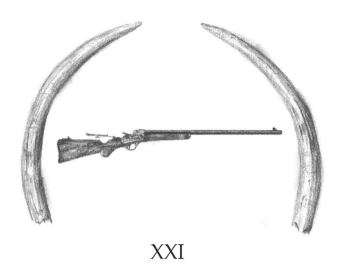

XXI

The large convoy of military supply trucks and crew carriers roll out across the remote African landscape. Midway along in the lineup of vehicles, the all-terrain Mercedes carrying Su Long Hang follows in the dusty path of the others. In total, six black-market military vehicles travel the rough-cut track through the brush to the projected site of the elephant herd.

Situated in the front passenger seat, Roosevelt looks back at Tusk who leans against the rear driver-side door with his hands tied to the safety handle overhead. She cranes her neck around to Su Long Hang who sits directly behind her and casually aims his pistol at the restrained hunter. Her eyes travel back to connect with Tusk's and she shakes her head with disappointment.

"Is this what you call a rescue mission?"

His hands tied above his head, Tusk peers over at the pistol aimed at him and shrugs innocently.

"It's a work in progress."

Hang gives a laugh and waggles the pistol.

"You might not enjoy the next phase."

Tusk stares at Su Long Hang and smirks.

"You might not either."

The Chinese businessman returns the hard look at Tusk while keeping the pistol aimed. He clears his throat to speak slow and deliberate.

"You surely don't disappoint Mister Kalispell. From what I hear, you have earned the moniker 'Tusk', and even when all hope is lost, you still remain strangely optimistic. It will be a sad moment for Africa when you are properly eliminated."

Su Long Hang connects eyes with the driver in the rear-view mirror and responds with a nod.

"Face forward now, Madame Doctor. Otherwise you will miss the wonderful views."

The military style vehicles are parked in a makeshift camp as the workers unload supplies and set-up tents. Positioned in canvas folding chairs outside the largest tent, Tusk and Roosevelt sit tied, back to back. They watch the activity of the camp operation all around and Roosevelt looks over her shoulder at Tusk.

"This may be my first, but it seems like the worst thought-out rescue effort ever attempted."

Tusk tests his wrists against the secureness of the binding ropes on his wrists and flexes his back against the wood framed folding chair.

Africa Tusk

"Guess what? I haven't done this before either."

"Well, it hardly shows. What happens next?"

The safari hunter spots his longtime professional rival, Peter Logan, across the camp directing the native crew. The ill-fated circumstances of being at the mercenary's pleasure, fills Tusk with a mix of anger and shame.

"If we're lucky ... a lion or hyena will rush out of the tall grass and eat us. That way we won't have to answer any more questions to Logan or the Chinaman."

She turns her head and peers at him behind her.

"Nice plan."

Tusk continues to eye the camp and silently considers the number of men and existing guns. He murmurs the calculation to himself then interrupts his assessment to hiss over his shoulder at Roosevelt.

"Just remember, this is entirely your fault."

"How do you figure?"

"You got yourself abducted, remember?"

"I said it before; I should have stayed with you!"

"Well, now you are!"

They both stop arguing as they notice Su Long Hang walking over with Logan beside him. The Chinese businessman stops and stands before them with a smile.

"Are you two catching up nicely?"

Logan continues to move past Tusk and circles around to get a better view of Roosevelt. She squirms under his licentious stare as Tusk faces forward to confront Su Long Hang. The restrained hunter sits before the ivory poaching kingpin and shrugs.

"The machine you want is nowhere near here."

Su Long Hang nods agreeably and clasps his smallish hands behind his bush jacket.

"I figured that already. We have some harvesting business to attend first before we attempt to step into your imprudently laid trap."

Tusk stares ahead, innocently.

"What trap?"

"Yes, Mister Tusk, we are all very puzzled about your inane attempt at a rescue. What else could be the end result except to lure us to a pathetic bushwhack?"

Logan leans casually on the nearby tent pole and snorts.

"Nobody is that stupid."

Roosevelt nods over her shoulder toward her bound up companion and frowns.

"He may be ..."

With his small hands still clasped at his backside, Su Long Hang stares ahead and shakes his head.

"That is highly unlikely. We will have to figure out his strategy another way."

Tusk turns back toward Roosevelt and grimaces at her obvious lack of faith in him. Their gazes connect for a moment and he returns to face forward after receiving an obnoxious roll of her eyes. Hang stares curiously at the captured pair and Tusk forces a grin before speaking.

"I was relying on you being a man of honor. I offered a deal of fair trade ... the weapon for her."

The Chinaman snickers maniacally and circles the two hostages secured in the wooden camp chairs. His jowls jiggle as he murmurs aloud in his distinctive use of the English language.

Africa Tusk

"Americans are most entertaining with their sense of honor and fair-play in conducting business transactions. It is laughable to me how they use it as an apology for stupidity."

Peter Logan takes his yearning stare off Roosevelt a moment to glare at Su Long Hang as he continues his discourse on the foolishness of Americans.

"Out here in the darkest of Africa, there is no place for morality in business. You take what you want in this world and let the dead have the honorable path. That is why America is now failing and my country is prospering from their defectors of industry."

Tusk interrupts under his breath.

"It's because we're honorable?"

"No ... because you Americans pamper the weak. Your country is run by an oversized political machine that encourages entitlement of the poor and lazy ... those who will suck at the teat of government until it brings everyone down to the welfare class. In my country, we have a strong force of worker-ants that do the jobs that need doing or they starve to death. Their honor comes from hard labor, not empty words of promise."

Roosevelt catches Logan's strange look of contempt toward Hang and watches him until his lustful attentions turn back toward her. She clears her throat and looks over at the Chinese businessman.

"I'm from England."

Hang detects the mercenary hunter's interest, standing over the doctor and giggles with amusement.

"Don't even get me started on the British."

Su Long Hang continues his circling pace and pauses to stand before Tusk.

"You can tell us of your little scheme now or we can flush it out of you by force later."

An expression of curious dread passes over the safari hunter as he looks to Logan and back at Hang.

"Flush it out of me?"

Hang nods affirmative.

"Waterboarding is a finely tuned motivator for extracting the information we need. You have to thank the Japs for its pervasive use during the World War."

"Thank the Japanese, huh?"

"Did you think they only developed cars?"

Tusk shrugs with a snorting reply.

"How about fair trade?"

Hang shakes his head and looks up to the afternoon sky.

"No deal. I already have you both and it's just a matter of time until I get what I want. You cannot hide things here in Africa, she always whispers her secrets."

He waves over two tribesmen with machine guns, utters directives to them in Somali then smiles grimly down at Tusk and Roosevelt.

"I will keep you around for the harvest tomorrow and then kill you unless you conjure up a reason not to."

Tusk grunts dejected.

"Thanks, that gives us something to think about."

"And think about it you should."

Su Long Hang ushers Logan away to the provisional headquarters and Roosevelt sighs as she looks around at their unfortunate situation. The two guards stand and smoke in the fading light of the late afternoon sky.

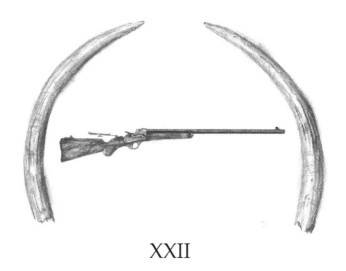

XXII

Darkness consumes the shadows between the burning kerosene lanterns positioned around the poacher camp. The two captives remain tied to portable chairs, secured back to back. Roosevelt stares into the blackness of night and hears the hinted sounds of slumber from the man seated directly behind her. His breaths become longer and his head occasionally droops and tilts to the side.

Roosevelt rattles her hands against the chair back and Tusk's nodding head jerks up alert. She watches the attending guards, a short distance away and speaks in a sharp, hissing whisper over her shoulder.

"Are you sleeping?"

"I was about to."

"What the hell's wrong with you?"

Tusk sniffs and glances over his shoulder at her.

"Nothing, I'm just tired."

The wooden chairs creak as Roosevelt does her best to twist toward the man secured behind her.

"Don't you see a problem with that?"

"Other than being tied to a chair with you?"

"How are we going to escape?"

The words of the exasperated female seem to carry farther than intended in the quiet camp and Tusk tenses in his seat behind her. His eyes dart to the guards, lounging in the shadows, with their guns a few feet away and he whispers to her in a lower tone.

"We're not."

"What?"

"They plan to kill us tomorrow. Any rash escape attempt will only force their hand to murder us sooner."

Roosevelt arches her back, turns forward and grumbles as she stares into the consuming darkness.

"So what's your solution to our situation?"

"Get some rest."

She takes a deep breath and huffs with agitation.

"You're useless."

With an amused shrug, Tusk closes his eyes.

"It seems I've got my hands tied on this one."

Nocturnal sounds echo through the settled camp as Roosevelt silently fumes with anger. Drifting clouds shroud the stars overhead and Tusk bows his head to drift off into an exhausted slumber. She listens to the chatter of the nighttime surroundings pause and hears someone approach on foot from behind. A shiver of panic passes over as she hears a deep familiar voice.

"Hey sweetheart ..."

Africa Tusk

Peter Logan puts his palm to the back of her head and strokes his fingers down along her neckline. His heavy outdoor scent is upon her as he rests his groping hand on her tensed shoulder. She sits dreadfully still and cringes when he moves around the chair to face her.

"You awake, darling?"

Roosevelt turns a probing ear toward Tusk and listens to him softly snoring.

The mercenary hunter looms above and turns her chin back toward him. His hot breath with the smell of homegrown whiskey burns her senses and makes her body recoil. He lowers his face to hers and speaks.

"I have a winning proposition for you."

Despite his powerful grip on her jaw, Roosevelt tries to muster up all of her remaining courage. The slightly intoxicated hunter stares coolly with black, glossed over eyes that reflect the twin lamplights hung nearby. Roosevelt replies in a loud exaggerated tone, hoping to wake the body behind her or make someone in the camp take notice.

"Mister Logan, I'm sure you have your ideas!"

The startled expression on Logan's face turns to amusement as her showy response receives no results.

"Shh, honey … no need to wake anyone else."

The true aloneness of her situation brings on a hollow feeling and she remains quiet until Logan speaks again.

"You want to get out of here alive, Darlin'?"

Her nerves begin to show as he tilts her head back and her lip quivers uncontrollably.

"Don't you have to answer to your boss?"

Logan's glassy eyes travel over to the watching guards and he gestures a shooing wave. They nod obedient and promptly turn their backs to the encounter.

"These are my local boys who work the camp … you heard his inspired talk about morality and misspent honor. I have no loyalty to that Chinaman, only to the money he pays."

Roosevelt's mind reels as she tries to conceal emotions.

"You can get me out of here?"

"I can do anything … for a price."

She thinks then nods over her shoulder at Tusk.

"How about sleeping beauty behind me here?"

Logan stands erect and his wide torso obscures the glowing lamplight that plays across Roosevelt's features. He shakes his head slowly and talks in a low, gravely whisper.

"Lady, you may be a mite pretty and have some unique assets, but you don't got what it takes to save him from what's comin'. Us two have a long history and his life ain't worth squat to me anymore."

Logan shifts and the lantern light returns to her features.

"Don't you worry none … he's crafty enough to fend for himself. Now, if you don't want a bullet put in your brainpan tomorrow, please consider my offer."

The mercenary hunter reaches out and puts his hand gently under her chin. He holds it a moment then bends closer and gives her a scratchy, whisker-stubble caress with his lips. He pulls back with a smiling wink and she returns the gesture by spitting into his face.

Laughing faintly, Logan wipes his chin slow then lashes out with a strong backhand to Roosevelt's cheek.

Her head turns violently to the side and she chokes back the throbbing pain of the blow with a quiet whimper. The menacing figure grabs her by a fistful of hair and talks gruffly into her turned ear.

"I do like a little spunk in my gals. You're the best looking piece of white meat I've seen in a long time. It would be a shame to see it go to waste."

He scans his eyes around the silent camp and the turned away guards. He releases her hair and pats his hand to the top of her head playfully. The light from the oil lantern glimmers on his hard features as his stern demeanor cracks into a wicked grin.

"Think about it. It could be worse."

"I can't even imagine."

A grim seriousness returns over his countenance.

"Believe me … one attentive animal is much better than being ravaged by twenty hungry beasts."

Logan steps away and chatters some hushed orders to the nearby guards. They resume their watch over the prisoners as the mercenary hunter disappears into the obscurity of night. Left in a cold chill of terror, Roosevelt looks out to the edge of darkness.

The camp slowly wakes in the early light of morning. The sounds of nocturnal activity shift as the purple-black sky turns to shades of faded blue. Tusk gradually awakens, uncomfortable in the chair, still tied to Roosevelt seated behind him. Her body leans forward against the constraints in an awkward sleeping slump. He studies the camp through nearly closed eyelids and tracks the movements of the men around the trucks.

After speaking with an arriving native, the armed tribesmen, holding automatic rifles, march toward the secured hostages and one of them draws a skinning blade from his belt sheath. Tusk reaches back and gives Roosevelt's hand a forceful squeeze to urge her awake.

"Look alive, Doctor, this may be it!"

The dark-skinned tribesman with the knife slings his rifle over one shoulder and reaches out toward the captives. As the gleaming blade draws nearer, Tusk's body coils like a tensed spring readying to give the last battle for life. The knife slashes forward and neatly cuts the prisoner's ties at the wrists and torso.

Tusk leaps to his feet and stands with clenched fists raised, ready to engage. The two poachers look at him with a queer sense of surprised shock. Roosevelt rises from her chair and drops the severed ropes to the ground. A moment of misunderstanding transpires as the tribesman with the automatic rifle raises it at Tusk and breaks into a wide, teeth-bearing grin.

In heavyily accented English, the native man with the machine gun speaks.

"You have been summoned."

The other armed man motions his gun at Roosevelt who turns to Tusk for some sort of answer. Tusk shrugs and lowers his relaxed hands.

"I guess we follow them."

She nods and kicks the loosed ropes away from her ankles. Both gunman gesture their automatic rifles and usher the pair toward the center of camp. Tusk steps forward and glances at Roosevelt beside him. He gives her a deliberate scan and whispers.

Africa Tusk

"What happened to your eye?"

Roosevelt brushes her fingers past her bruised cheekbone and tries not to show any sign of weakness.

"I guess you slept through all the fun last night. I can hardly wait to find out what you have planned for us next on this glorious adventure."

The lady doctor inhales a deep self-assured breath and marches on ahead in front of the armed natives. Tusk tilts his head confused and follows along, ever curious about the unfolding state of affairs.

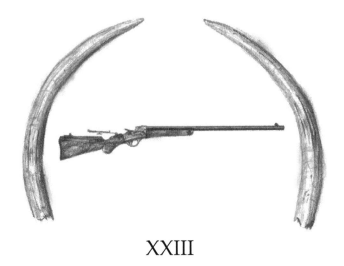

XXIII

Along the perimeter of the harvesting camp, trucks are lined up and ready to move out. Su Long Hang stands next to his armored Mercedes SUV and waves his gun at the crew, directing it as a persuasive pointer. He grins satisfied as the two captives are escorted toward him.

The Chinese businessman's dark, narrow eyes instantly spot the rosy discoloration on Roosevelt's upper cheek as she is brought before him. His eyes suspiciously dart to Tusk standing alongside her and he inquires with tempered distain.

"Rough night? No plans for escape, I hope?"
Roosevelt touches her tender eye self-consciously and looks away. Tusk scratches the back of his neck while observing the heavily armed hunting party.

"Depends. When are you planning to kill us?"

Africa Tusk

Hang lets a snicker escape from his thin lips and tucks his pistol along the front waistband of his trousers.

"I may keep you around a bit longer just for your entertainment value."

The amused Chinaman rattles off a command and one of the nearby tribesmen jumps forward to open the rear passenger door on the Mercedes all-terrain vehicle. Su Long Hang offers a small bow and ushers the pair inside.

"Mister Tusk, you first please."

"What happened to ladies first?"

"Let's just say you will be the first to leave us."

Su Long Hang smiles with glee as the two are escorted forward and step aboard. Before Hang climbs inside, the pistol is drawn from his pants waist and he prods Roosevelt to scoot along the rear bench seat of the armored vehicle.

"Skootch over a bit and make some room for me. It's time to go to work."

Su Long Hang follows into the waiting SUV and the door is secured behind him. All the vehicles begin to roll ahead and the convoy, containing native men, guns and poaching supplies, travels out of camp in unison.

Positioned in the back middle seat, Roosevelt stares forward out the front windscreen. The dark-skinned driver watches over the steering wheel as the musical beat of low volume rhumba tunes emit from the car radio. She looks to Tusk next to her who watches quietly out the side window, then to Hang who taps away swiftly at the lighted screen of his cellular phone.

Alone with her thoughts, Roosevelt watches the dust trail rise and roll to the side from the truck tires traveling ahead. An overwhelming sadness for her own precarious condition and for the imperiled elephants surges through her. The selecting ping of handheld electronics pulls her from her morose musings.

Roosevelt again watches Su Long Hang while he scrolls through messages on his phone and taps replies. She peers down at the glowing screen but the jumble of foreign typescript in the text is unintelligible.

"What are you going to do when the elephants are gone and there is no more ivory to take?"
Su Long Hang taps a final message on his phone, presses send and tucks it away.

"I guess I will retire a very wealthy man."

"With the death of a species on your head?"
He turns with a dark twinkle of mystique in his gaze.

"Despite my efficiency and success, I am not the only vendor of ivory. The worldwide demand is much too great for me alone to satisfy the market. Besides, doing what one enjoys can push a lot of death, misery and consequences to the back of a person's thoughts. Isn't that right, Mister Tusk?"

Tusk breaks his silent trance from the tinted view out the side window and raises a curious eyebrow.

"Are you comparing me to you?"

"We are both hunters, are we not?"
The professional safari hunter grunts disagreeably.

"I would hardly call what you do hunting."

"The end result is the same. I just make it much more profitable."

Africa Tusk

Tusk gives a melancholy shake of his head.

"You're a murdering lunatic."

"Wrong … I am an international businessman who harvests natural resources and supplies a lucrative market in Asia. You merely kill exotic animals to supply sport trophies to a few rich gentlemen with Hemingway complexes."

Su Long Hang wipes the beading sweat from his around his mouth and smiles at Roosevelt as he continues.

"Who is more right? I serve the needs of millions and he serves only the few with millions to spend."

Roosevelt silently observes the two men on either side of her. The cool air from the car vents lessens the damp humidity. Tusk gazes out the window at a herd of zebra trotting away and a single word escapes his lips.

"Respect …"

The Chinaman leans forward in his seat, staring at Tusk.

"How is that?"

"I show others to hunt with a respect for the animal and the continuance of a species. We stalk an animal at twenty meters where you connect with the life and soul you're about to take away or be taken by."

Su Long Hang slaps his knee and laughs while turning his amused countenance to Roosevelt.

"Respectful is it … to mount a victim's head on the wall to gawk at? I know for a fact that your new friend here puts himself much farther away than that when using his big gun on unsuspecting victims."

Seated between, Roosevelt adds to the conversation.

"Men who use machine guns, chain saws and hatchets on animals have no soul worth seeing."

Eric H. Heisner

Tusk watches out the window and mumbles low.

"When I kill you … I'll mount your head over the crapper in the outhouse."

Hang continues to giggle with amusement.

"Aww, Mister Tusk. You Americans always are jesting and good for a laugh."

Focusing his whole attention on the attractive doctor, Su Long Hang puts his hand to her upper thigh. She shrinks back, but he holds tight as he leans closer to her reddened cheek.

"And what are your cultured thoughts my dear? I suppose you are a member to the community of devout lacto-intolerant vegans who will eat the organic foliage away from our livelihood."

She swats his hand from her leg as he laughs.

"At the rate people are killing off the elephant population, they will be extinct in less than a decade."

The Chinese businessman wrings his slender hands together and grins at her.

"You are obviously an idealistic conservationist and not business-minded. Yes, a sad tear will fall for the loss of the large beasts but I will be able to wipe the grief away with the exorbitant amounts of money people will pay for my stockpile from the rarest of creatures."

A look of horror fills Roosevelt's features.

"You're trying to kill them off?"

"Simple, supply and demand my Dearie."

"That's disgusting."

Hang shrugs in a matter of fact way.

"Elephant ivory will be sought after like diamonds someday and I will have the inventory."

Africa Tusk

The thought of the blatant animal butchering leaves Roosevelt aghast and she is conflicted as to where to turn so the two men won't see her tears. Suddenly the trucks stop and the dust from the tires swirl around and over the halted vehicles. Ahead, a large herd of farm cattle moves slowly across the path of the trucks and seems to spread out and consume the stopped caravan.

The slow moving animals are guided by a dozen native ranchers in sandaled feet with herding staffs to direct the general route of travel. Several of the dusty tribesmen move close to the vehicle convoy and peer curiously into the truck windows. A shadowed figure passes by Hang's window and cups his hands around his face to peer inside past his own mirrored reflection.

The probing eyes make for an uncomfortable image in the window until Hang raps his knuckles on the tinted glass and hollers ahead to the driver.

"Why are we stopping for this? Get us moving!" The driver picks up his handheld radio and chatters urgently into it. After a long moment, the sounds of engines revving comes from ahead in the line and the trucks before them begin to slowly roll forward again.

Tusk watches out the darkened window while several herdsmen stand along the roadside, staring toward him as if they could actually see through the shaded glass. The vehicle rolls past the figure at Hang's window and nudges through the milling livestock. Shifting in the middle seat, Roosevelt leans over to Tusk and half-whispers.

"Who are they?"

"Samburu ...

Hang interrupts with a huff and shakes off the visual of the unnerving occurrence at his window.

"They are cattle and livestock raisers my dear. I'm afraid your hopes for a valiant rescue will not materialize as they are a peaceful tribe who don't often find the need to hunt."

Tusk shakes his head dismissive.

"They have no love for poachers."

Hang sighs at the window impatiently as the caravan sluggishly creeps through the slow-moving cattle.

"Actually nobody does, but they have their little protected area and we only cull the animals that stray from the reaches of their watchful eyes. Some of them even silently encourage the removal of the elephants for their own grazing purposes."

A look of disgust clouds Tusk's features and he continues to stare out the window at the passing mob of domestic forage animals.

"How much farther are we going?"

"We should be spotting the herd in an hour."

Roosevelt sits hushed between the two men as they continue to converse with a hostile undercurrent.

"How are you thinking you will get the ivory out through the Samburu reservation?"

Hang grins smugly.

"Shooting our helicopter out of the sky may have seemed like clever work to you, but it only served as a small delay in the operation. We will fly out the more valuable pieces and truck the rest away as an expendable decoy that may or may not get through the border."

Africa Tusk

"Fly it right into Mombasa, huh? How much does that cost you in official bribes?"

"All money well spent and merely a write-off."

Positioned between the two as they trade words, Roosevelt seems shocked at how candid and informative the Chinese capitalist is being. She turns to face Su Long Hang and forces a pleasant appearance.

"Would you care to provide names?"

Su Long Hang laughs giddily and pats her knee.

"I would gladly, but that could only give you a false hope for both of your survival."

Tusk looks down at the bindings around his wrists and gauges the short distance to throttling the Chinaman's neck. He flexes his hands painfully as Roosevelt takes over the conversation.

"To kill us is an incredible waste of opportunity when there are many things we could be useful for?"

Hang nods agreeable.

"Mister Tusk has proven he can be very amusing and his local status around the bush is almost legendary, but you ... I would have to question your loyalty."

"I could be loyal."

Su Long Hang smiles and turns forward.

"Aww, women and their lies."

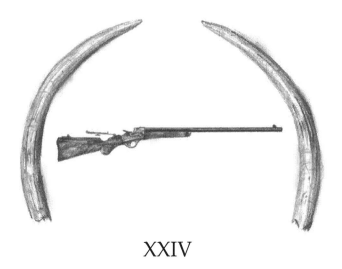

XXIV

The convoy of military-looking vehicles pulls up to the edge of a valley with a wide view of a watering hole in the distance. The shrill sounds and grunts of several elephants frolicking are heard as the oversized animals roll and play in the communal mud hole that spreads to marshy grassland. Perched atop one of the truck cabs, a single, lean native roosts while peering through a set of binoculars, taking a head count of the herd.

The interior of Su Long Hang's SUV is a-chatter with unintelligible voices coming from the handheld radio. Tusk stares out the dark window, watching the elephants on the horizon while his temper burns hot under his calm exterior. Both Roosevelt and Tusk notice as Peter Logan approaches the vehicle with two of his rifle carrying crewmen. Su Long Hang lowers the window and eagerly asks for a report from Logan.

Africa Tusk

"How big of a herd is it?"

"They're getting a head count on the ivory now. The chopper is due at zero six hundred tomorrow."

Logan looks across the interior of the vehicle to Tusk at the opposite door who meets his steely gaze.

"A chunk of lead was found in the tail rotor … that seemed to cause the mechanical problem."

The Chinese businessman at the window nods to Logan and makes mental calculations for the harvest while tapping his fingers on his knee.

"Fine … fine. Set up the camp for the night and bee fences on the exiting paths along the perimeter. Let me know the exact count on ivory as soon as you get it."

Roosevelt turns to Tusk and whispers.

"What's a bee fence?"

"A string of hives across the migration path … one of the few things the big animals are afraid of."

The mercenary hunter at the window leans in slightly and catches Roosevelt's eye with a knowing wink. She quickly glances away and he smiles cocksure as he speaks to Su Long Hang.

"What are you wanting me to do with them?"

His attention now on his cell phone, Su Long Hang punches several buttons and snorts.

"Stash them away until after the job is done."

"With pleasure."

Logan smiles as he rolls his fingers on the door frame alongside the open window. Ignoring his wolfish grin, Roosevelt speaks aside to Su Long Hang.

"What then, Mister Hang?"

The Chinaman turns his attention to her, interrupting his task on the phone. The light from the illuminated pad glows brightly on his features in the tinted interior.

"You will be left behind and made to appear responsible for the brutal and disgraceful carnage. It will make a pretty photograph for the International Press having a protector of animals caught with a chainsaw in hand, standing over a defaced elephant."

"How would that help your cause?"

"When driving up the market price of rare commodities, they say any press is good press."

Tusk shakes his head and stares out to the distant watering hole while the thought of the gruesome setup sends chills down Roosevelt's spine.

"You couldn't make me do it."

"Madame… where I am from, we can make you do anything we please with the right persuasion."
Logan laughs and steps back from the window.

"Heck, you'd be easy compared to some."
Hang nods in agreement.

"Women seem to be much easier to manipulate, perhaps due to a bigger heart to break or a greater imagination for what we might actually do."

The rear passenger window rolls up to fleeting darkness until the door is opened, letting the daylight stream in again. Su Long Hang tucks his phone in his jacket and steps outside. He tucks his pistol into another pocket and looks from Tusk to Logan.

"Make sure they are well guarded and kept from any mischief. I don't want them to miss out on the big exciting plans we have for them in the morning."

Africa Tusk

Stepping aside from the doorway, Logan watches as Hang walks away toward the shade of the trees with the two bodyguards in tow. The mercenary hunter swings into the opening and hangs from the top of the open car door. He stares inside at Roosevelt and Tusk seated in the SUV and moves his hand along the seat.

"Well, let's get you both stashed away. Like the Chinaman said ... big day tomorrow."

A kerosene lantern hangs in to the corner of a sparsely furnished tent, illuminating the canvas walls. In the middle of the sheltered space on a low leather-slung chair, Roosevelt sits alone with her hands lashed tight. She apprehensively watches and listens to every shadow and sound that passes outside the tent.

The front flap suddenly swings open and the dark glistening face from one of her assigned guards appears inside. His white-blinking eyes look around the tent interior a moment then he steps back and holds the door canvas wide. Another guard pushes Tusk forward into the tent then prods him aggressively with the broadside of his rifle. Hands secured behind his back, Tusk stumbles and hits the ground with a heavy thud.

Roosevelt moves her feet away as Tusk rolls aside to get his face off the ground. She looks down at him in the dim flickering light of the tent.

"Are you okay?"

Tusk spits trampled grass away from his mouth.

"No, I'm not ... thanks for askin'."

She peers up at their captors as they laugh between themselves and flip the canvas tent door closed.

After some wiggling and grunting, Tusk manages to maneuver himself to a sitting position. The lamplight flickers off the hunter's features to reveal a beat up and bloodied grimace. Roosevelt looks down at Tusk from the chair as he sits upright.

"What did they ask?"

"Nothing they didn't already know the answer."

"We need to get out of here."

He flexes his hands and arms behind his back and tries to get more comfortable in the restraints.

"Yeah, can't you see I'm working on it?" Tusk spits a smear of dark mucus on the canvas wall.

"Logan is coming for you next ..."

The tent flap swings open, as if on cue and Logan stands with the guards, holding a light aimed to the interior.

"Did I hear mention of my name?"

Tusk clears the blood draining from his nasal passage and hacks it away with a grunt.

"That or I just crapped in my pants? I may have lost some control after the fifth round of questioning."

Logan shines the lighted beam on Tusk's battered features and steps inside the tent a short distance from the figure propped up on the ground. He switches hands with the flashlight and sneers at his old adversary.

"Always the jokester ... eh, Tusk?"

His gnarled fist quickly strikes out and smashes the seated hunter along the upper cheekbone sending him against the forgiving canvas wall of the tent.

Tusk flops over and looks back with a confined rage while Roosevelt struggles in her chair and shouts.

"Stop it you ..."

Logan quickly pivots and gives her a backhand across the mouth before she can finish her outburst. He holds up a pointed finger and wags it as she gingerly touches her tongue to her tingling lips.

"Watch your words or I may lose my temper."

Roosevelt looks up at him and attempts to control her combination of fear and anger. Logan glares at Tusk on the ground and turns back to Roosevelt as he speaks over his shoulder to the guard behind.

"Go ahead and loose her from the chair."

One of the armed men moves forward, slings his rifle over his shoulder and unties her from the chair. Logan reaches out his hand in a generous offering of help.

With her arms liberated, Roosevelt rubs her wrists and reaches to accept Logan's outstretched hand. She places her right palm in his, grips tight and lashes out with the clenched ball of her left fist. Her compact knuckles smash under Logan's broad jowl and his chin snaps upward. In a daze, he shakes off the unexpected jolt and she promptly jabs him again in the nose.

His vision momentarily blurred, Logan clamps down on her small hand and swings his arm around to club her awkwardly across the shoulder. Her slender frame topples from the powerful blow and she tumbles next to Tusk alongside the canvas wall. Logan still holds a twisting grip on her wrist as he gingerly touches a faint trickle of blood from his reddened snout. He sniffs sharply while swiping a thick finger along a nostril then shakes his head at her.

"You like it rough? I can give it to you rough ..."

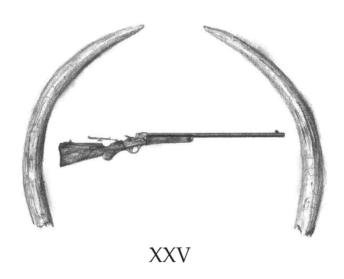

XXV

The raucous sounds of night consume the darkness and the faint murmurs of elephants can be heard in the far distance. The camp of poacher trucks and tents is mostly docile with several campfires flickering highlights on multiple stacks of guns leaned up in teepee fashion. The lethal AK-47 auto rifles stand with stocks circled on the ground and barrels entwined.

From his laid down position on the dirt floor inside the tent, Tusk rolls back from peering under the canvas wall and looks around the dimly lit interior. The single chair remains unoccupied and the prone hunter watches the cast shadows of the guards at the front entrance. With hands tied behind his back, Tusk strains against the bonds around his wrists then lies back in a huff of breath. A rustle at the rear of the tent catches his attention and he arches back to see what type of animal he might fall victim to.

The bottom edge of the canvas rises slightly and Tusk scoots his body around in an attempt to better defend himself from the night creature. Surprisingly, the welcome face of Mogambo appears peering under the lifted tent side. The dark skinned figure flashes a toothy smile when he spots Tusk alone in the tent and the bound hunter sighs and grunts under his breath.

"About damn time …"

The thin frame of Mogambo slides under the tent wall and moves silently to Tusk's side. A knife flashes in the shadowy light and he cuts the ties away from Tusk's wrists and whispers.

"You always say, better late than never."
Tusk brings his arms around to the front and shakes the bindings from his hands. He rubs the rope marked skin, flexes his fingers and climbs to his feet.

A quick glance to the front entry and Tusk speaks quietly to Mogambo.

"Logan has Roosevelt."
A slight shake from the gun bearer's head and Mogambo crouches low and moves to the rear of the tent.

"No, Bwana … follow me."

"What do you mean, No?"
At the back wall of the tent, Mogambo quietly lifts the canvas barrier and eases back under.

The small gap along the ground remains open as the loyal native waits outside. The lounging shadows of the guards remain unmoved at the taut canvas entrance. Tusk glances toward the front of the tent and slips away.

The night is dark and almost starless as a haze of fog settles over the camp. Tusk follows closely behind Mogambo through the cool night air and senses they are headed wide of the location where he was previously questioned. They skirt the edges of the camp and pause in the shadows as they encounter several men on patrol.

Nearly to the opposite side of the camp, Tusk reaches out a hand and places it on the shoulder of his trusted guide. Mogambo turns to him and his eyes blink in the night as he puts a quiet finger to his lips. He motions to a tent not far ahead and they quietly move around the side to the rear panel.

The two figures slip under the back wall of the tent and Tusk quickly assesses the interior in the dim lantern light. The body of a man lies trussed on the floor and Tusk looks to the opposite corner and sees the shadowy form of Roosevelt with a pistol in her hand. Tusk lets his eyes adjust to the low light and moves around to see his old adversary, Logan, bound and gagged on the floor. The two rivals let their eyes connect in a mutual disdain of antipathy.

He looks up to Roosevelt as she steps forward and notices her abused features and a dark smear under her nose. She looks ill at ease, standing before him with the gun still cocked and pointed at Logan. The dwelling is silent as Tusk reaches out and places his hand over the pistol, lowering it and removing it from her grasp.

He engages the handgun's safety and tucks it behind in his waistband. Roosevelt wipes the back of her hand across her cheek and smears the trickle of blood from her nostril. She stares down at the tied man on the floor as conflicted emotions of relief and hatred swell uncontrollably over her.

A comforting arm wraps around her shoulder and Tusk pulls her close in embrace. With soft, quiet overwhelming sobs, Roosevelt buries her head in his chest and murmurs low.

"He said you were dead and would do the same to me if I didn't cooperate. He was going to ..."
Tusk clenches her tight and murmurs low in her ear.

"It's okay ... we're alive yet."
Finally, she regains control of her emotions and looks up.

"How will we ever get away from here?"
"We'll manage somehow."

Tusk holds Roosevelt close to his chest and smoothes his hand across her back. Letting his eyes wander toward Mogambo, he probes the question to his friend with his questioning gaze. The loyal native scout shakes his head and squats down on the floor by the canvas door flap, looking out.

The hour of night passes on and the dim interior of the mercenary hunter's canvas dwelling burns with low lantern light. Peter Logan lies hog-tied in the center of the matted grass floor. Behind him, on a folding cot, Roosevelt lies curled with her arms crossed on her chest seemingly calm and attempting rest. Tusk kneels in the far corner near the entrance with Mogambo and speaks in hushed whispered tones.

"You don't think we could make it out clear?"
"Not in the way I came, Bwana."

Tusk peers out of the tent and spots two guards on night patrol and then another figure just outside the perimeter of the clustered camp.

"It won't be long before daylight and they'll discover us missing. The area will be turned inside out until they find us."

Mogambo nods and watches out past the dispersed glow of lanterns into the dark void.

"I spoke with Maasai and Samburu."

"Together? What did they say?"

"They try ... might get us away."

"Which tribe?"

"If not one, then the other."

Tusk looks out at the many stacks of automatic rifles.

"They are no match for these kinds of weapons."

The tent flap held close to his features, Mogambo nods solemnly. Tusk turns and looks behind at Logan on the floor and Roosevelt curled on the folding cot.

"You have any other ideas?"

Mogambo watches expressionlessly out into the night.

"We wait, Bwana."

"How?"

The native companion continues to stare out with an empty expression into the shrouded surroundings of the poacher camp.

"With patience, my friend."

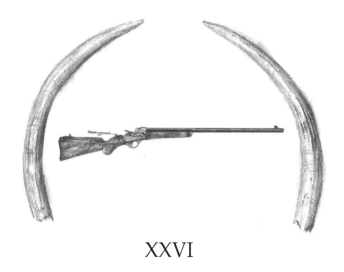

XXVI

The sky begins to brighten and a chill sweeps the air with the coming of daybreak. Echoing sounds from nocturnal creatures recede as the heavy mist rises from the tall grass in the surrounding marshland. Several machine gun bearing night guards rise from their concealed position in the brush and take brisk circular steps to ease their cramped legs.

The entry tent flap to Peter Logan's quarters wavers with movement then closes. The lamp light inside is still turned low as Tusk passes a worried look to Mogambo then draws Logan's automatic pistol from his pant waist. He turns the pistol on its side and quietly ejects the magazine from the handgrip. Tusk counts the available rounds in the loaded clip before sliding it back into place with a solid click.

Tusk winces at the distinct clatter of the readied firearm while he and Mogambo observe approaching movement outside the tent. They wait apprehensively at the entry as two native tribesmen walk past Logan's dwelling and tilt their heads toward the canvas shell, listening with curiosity. The one guard softly speaks to the other and they snicker quietly while strolling away with automatic rifles still slung over shoulders.

Inside the tent, both men exhale a relieved breath and Tusk puts his hand gently to Mogambo's arm.

"We don't have any more time. We have to go."
The trustworthy scout peers outside with a sharp eye and turns to Tusk, shaking his head again.

"We wait, Bwana."

"This tent is no place to defend and we can't hold for daylight if we want to make it clear of this camp."
The tracker raises an open palm to signal quiet and a slight reverberating tremor is felt through the ground.

"Very soon, opportunity come."

A moment passes and Tusk starts to feel the stronger rumbling sensation come up from the bottom of his boot soles. He looks quizzically at his native friend.

"What is that?"
The native man grins and grips his readied knife.

"Thems our chance for escape."

A strange surge of energy charges the damp, misty air as the bellows from a Samburu cattle herd breaks the stillness of morning. Tusk peers outside and sees several head of livestock racing toward the camp.

"Stampede?"

Africa Tusk

Mogambo nods as he crouches, ready to spring out the doorway. The whole earth seems to rumble more intensely and Tusk rushes to Roosevelt's side and rouses her from sleep. She sits up on the cot, feeling the thundering cadence of pounding hooves and plants her feet on the trembling ground.

"What is it, the elephants?"

"A cattle stampede and our ticket out!"

Tusk pulls Roosevelt to her feet and they step over Peter Logan, still tied on the grassy floor. At the front entrance, the safari hunter releases his hold on her hand and returns to stand over his restrained adversary. The bound and gagged mercenary fixes angry eyes up at Tusk, questioning his intentions. The former captive tilts his chin and flashes a sly grin at Logan.

"I may not get another chance like this."

Logan cocks his head inquisitively and Tusk hauls off and plants a swift booted kick to the trussed man's midsection. In wheezing gasps, Logan blows air out through the mouth gag. Tusk leans down, grabs Logan by the collar and turns his head so they are face to face. A mutual dislike emanates from their features.

"I ever find you in my sights at another massacre and you'll have a lead-slug-ticket to the gates of hell!"

Logan sucks for breath through the gag kerchief over his mouth and flares his nostrils. The mercenary's eyes blaze with hostility as Tusk looks over his shoulder toward Mogambo and Roosevelt at the tent's entry flap, ready to depart. Tusk lowers the bound man slightly to the ground when a distant elephant trumpet turns him back with a sudden burst of angry rage.

At the center of the tent, crouched low on the floor, Everett 'Tusk' Kalispell stares hard into Logan's dark, unrepentant eyes. The fingers on his hands clench together into tight fists wanting to exact payment for past transgressions. Mogambo utters something at the tent entry and Roosevelt whispers loudly.

"C'mon, let's go!"

The increased rumbling of the surrounding terrain makes the hanging kerosene lantern rattle and flicker as Tusk glares intently at Logan. Mogambo is halfway out the door with Roosevelt close behind him. The mercenary hunter cracks a wicked grin and grunts through the restrictive mouth gag.

"You'll never make it away from this camp alive. Your efforts won't even make a difference?"

Tusk reflects a short second then smashes his clenched fist into Logan's smug face. He raises his trembling fist again but restrains himself and releases the dazed man to the ground. The bellows of running cattle surround the area and the camp become alive with the sounds of panicked confusion.

Mogambo holds aside the tent flap and peers back at Tusk kneeled over the bound mercenary.

"We go now, Bwana."

Dashing for the doorway, Tusk grabs Roosevelt by the arm and follows Mogambo out the front opening.

The running, hooved stock consists of hundreds of horned cattle ripping through the canvas shelter camp and zig-zagging around parked vehicles and equipment. Stacks of automatic rifles tumble aside and are crushed by the rushing herd of beeves. Weaving through the many obstacles, Mogambo nimbly escorts Tusk and Roosevelt away from the dangers of the camp. The unrelenting flow of charging animals increase and the camp is thick in a hustled blur of bellowing cowhide.

In the midst of the stampede, a surrounded tent collapses with wailing screams from the men trapped inside as they are trampled into the ground. Mogambo leaps to the sheltered protection of one of the trucks as Tusk and Roosevelt are cut off and pull back nearer to another parked vehicle. The lively sounds of chaos echo loudly as they watch the surge of animals rush past with various objects of debris snagged on stout pointed horns.

As Tusk and Roosevelt pull back from the flowing mass of cattle, a fugitive from the pandemonium slips from beneath the surrounded vehicle and creeps around the truck's front panel with a gun in hand. The native tribesman slowly creeps nearer until he reaches out and grabs ahold of Roosevelt's shoulder, pulling her away from Tusk's side. She yelps out a distress call into the roaring din of the stampede.

"Tusk … Help!"

Tusk quickly turns and is confronted by the lethal end of the assailant's firearm pointed directly at him. The shrewd captor backs away cautiously, holding Roosevelt as a shield while the flood of cattle continues to surround the idle vehicle. Held firm by her neck, Roosevelt is pulled to the forward wheels of the truck and the gunman peers over the hood as the animals continue to thunder past.

A hefty bull suddenly rams into the broadside of the vehicle, rocking it on its axle. The front wheels skid several feet sideways as another cloven footed beast gets its horn hung up on the edge of the brush guard. Tusk uses the diversion to lunge at the distracted hijacker, trying to wrestle the firearm from his grasp.

Catching them off balance, Roosevelt knocks the weapon from their hands and shoves the disarmed captor into the rushing crowd of animals. With the screaming tear of flesh and bone, the man is gored and trampled into the dry grassy ground. Roosevelt turns away from the gruesome sight and hugs in close to Tusk. He peers over the hood of the vehicle, and spots the trailing end of the thinning herd.

"The rush is almost passed, let's go!"

Their bodies squeezed together, Roosevelt grasps Tusks hand as he pulls her away from the smashed vehicle. The two fleeing figures weave through the last trailing cows as the fading roar of the stampede moves into the distance. They leap over downed tents and the wreckage of supplies as they rush to clear the circle of trucks before being detected by their captors as missing. At the edge of the trampled campsite, Tusk hurries Roosevelt across the open grassy field toward the concealment of the thicker brush and foliage.

Just before the tree line they are detained by two, machine gun carrying poachers and a man with head bent, kneeling on the ground between them. One of the poachers jabs his rifle into the hostage figure and the friendly face of Mogambo looks up at the pair. Tusk instantly raises Logan's automatic pistol, clicks off the safety and aims it at the nearest poacher then the other.

"Let him go!"

The two gunmen direct their attention beyond Tusk's shoulder to the ravaged camp and a strange air of supremacy crosses their countenances. A familiar accented voice comes from behind and both Tusk and Roosevelt instantly pivot toward the source.

"*No* ... don't let him go."

Su Long Hang steps from the broken assemblage of trucks and proceeds to walk toward them.

Appearing behind Hang are several tribesmen with their guns engaged and ready while more armed natives emerge on their flank. Tusk glances around and heaves a heavy sigh of disappointment when he sees Peter Logan step out into the clearing. Hang gestures nonchalantly with his pistol toward the weapon Tusk grips in his hand.

"Drop the firearm, Mister Kalispell."

Every poacher directs their aim at the pair, accompanied by the slapping rattle of hands on cocked and loaded receivers. Tusk slowly turns to Roosevelt, lowers the firearm and tosses it aside. The lady doctor stares incredulously at the surrendered safari hunter and shakes her head, disheartened.

"I do have to say ... you have the worst rescues."

The bellowing echo of herded cattle fades into the distance as the lone trumpet call of an elephant is heard. Su Long Hang stares at the recovered prisoners and clucks his tongue admonishingly.

"I would like to think this cattle dash was an unfortunate incident, but somehow I think you are both directly responsible."

Tusk glimpses down at the discarded firearm on the ground and reconsiders his options.

"Would you believe we were just stepping out to get some fresh air?"

Su Long Hang huffs a tired breath as he turns to Logan.

"Hardly, Mister Kalispell ... there has been a special appeal for the expediency of your demise. Since you have been a troublesome burden of late, I will acquiesce to Mister Logan."

Logan steps forward, next to Hang and smiles through yellow, blood-smeared teeth.

"You're all mine, pal ..."

Tusk shrugs dejected and looks from Roosevelt to Hang.

"Will you let the woman go?"

Hang holsters his pistol and offers a shake of his head as Logan takes another step closer. The mercenary hunter stares at Tusk then lets his gaze fall upon Roosevelt.

"I get a go at you first ... then it's her turn."

The sound of a low-flying helicopter thumping through the distant sky travels in the chill morning fog. Su Long Hang looks over to the eastern horizon as the sun crests the short rolling hills.

"Aww, right on time."

XXVII

The dark profile of the refurbished military helicopter flies low with the rising sun blazing in the orange firmament behind. It passes over the cattle-trampled campsite, circles high then hovers near the armed gathering at the edge of the forest line. Heads twist skyward and hands shield eyes to view the suspended chopper in the early light of daybreak.

The powerful rotary engine thumps whirling blades through the air as the helicopter hangs directly above. Debris churns and stirs upward from the ground as Su Long Hang signals with his hands for the chopper to land nearby. The hovering helicopter remains steady in the sky as lifted dust and dry tufts of grass swirl past the ground crew around broken tents flapping in the wind from the aircraft's wake.

The muted curses of Su Long Hang are lost in the airstream as his slicked hair stands hard against the air current and he repeatedly gestures where the helicopter should put down. Suddenly there is a burst of gunfire from the side cargo door and divots of earth explode from the ground. Several of the armed poachers standing behind Hang crumple to the ground with bullet hits from above. Without waiting for any explanation, Su Long Hang quickly runs for cover as another burst of gunfire is showered down on the armed assembly.

Along with the gathered crowd, Peter Logan gawks up at the belligerent chopper in dismayed shock. Tusk quickly takes the opportunity to step forward and swing at his rival with an uppercut of hammered fist. The smashing punch connects with Logan's upturned gazing jaw and lifts the mercenary hunter to his heels. Tusk follows up with another jab to the midsection and Logan flops to the ground in a gasping heap.

Another burst of gunfire from above scatters the confused observers and Tusk turns to Roosevelt, jabbing a finger toward the cover of trees.

"Go! Go there ..."

The helicopter above continues to rain down gunfire and Roosevelt stands immobile in the chaos. Tusk shoves her toward the shelter of the bush just as a group of Maasai warriors emerge into the early morning sunlight.

A poacher reaches out, catching Roosevelt by the shirtsleeve and a native hunting spear instantly skewers his abdomen. Shrieks of pain emit from the wounded poacher as he stares down at the long shaft entering his stomach. She shakes free from the clutching grip of her screaming attacker and stumbles toward the advancing warriors in full battle-dress costume.

One of the mercenaries standing over Mogambo catches a knife blade in the neck while the other grapples with the safari gun bearer on the ground. The scuffle quickly comes to an end when the poacher observes the fearsome tribe of Maasai warriors and flees to the shelter of the military trucks. Tusk grabs up a cast-off machine gun and chases after Roosevelt.

The sporadic gunfire from the helicopter above scatters everyone from the clearing. While running for the trees, Tusk glances up at the helicopter's attacking circle overhead. He trips and nearly tumbles when he catches an indication of the pilot's identity behind the controls. He regains his balance and blurts aloud in recognition of his old friend Butch wearing the headset.

"Holy crap ... Butch?"

Mogambo grabs at Tusk's arm to guide him and the two run for the tall brush, following after Roosevelt. At the edge of the clearing, Tusk gazes up at the chopper again before nodding a salute and spraying several rounds from the automatic rifle into the group of parked poacher vehicles. The whole area is a mass of machine-gun fire and confusion as bullets whiz in every direction. Keeping his head low, Mogambo parts the thick brush and ushers Roosevelt inside.

"We go now, Memsahib."

Roosevelt disappears into the vegetation cover and Mogambo calls to Tusk over the sounds of gunfire.

"Come now, Bwana!"

The rapid-fire machine gun in Tusk's hands lets off a few more short bursts which rattle and spark off the vehicle targets. He scans around then turns and dashes into the thick underbrush after Roosevelt and Mogambo.

The three escaping figures run crashing through the mix of tall grasses and scratching tangle of thicket. Ahead, Mogambo swiftly slides through the foliage as if it was his natural habitat. On his sandaled heels, the barbed branches and razor edges of coarse bladed grass seem to purposefully reach out and tear at the pair following. A whistling thorn branch scratches across Roosevelt's cheek and Tusk pushes her onward as she touches her hand across the shallow wound.

A mile away, the helicopter circles higher in the brightening sky and the sounds of continued blasts of gunfire resonance in the cool morning air. Traveling afoot, the three try to gain the maximum distance from the embattled poacher camp. They break into another grazed clearing and Roosevelt stops to catch her breath. Tusk takes a knee and carefully surveys their surroundings with the auto rifle cradled in his arms.

The warmer air of day begins to settle in as Mogambo stands; calmly taking shallow gulps of air. Far afield, a group of Cape buffalo stares inquisitively at the new arrivals. Tusk look around to other signs of wildlife as Roosevelt peers past her shoulder in the direction of intermittent pops of gunfire. She wipes sweat from her eyes while heaving air into her chest.

"What the hell was that?"

Africa Tusk

Tusk meets Mogambo's gaze with a tilt of his brow and they silently acknowledge their fortunate luck. Roosevelt astutely observes their exchange of glances and wipes the strands of hair from her face.

"Was that supposed to be a rescue? Who was in the helicopter and why was it shooting at everyone?" Mogambo's dark skin glistens with sweat and he nods.

"We is lucky, Memsahib."

"How was that lucky?"

The native scout flashes a gleaming smile to her.

"We is still alive."

Tusk stands straight with the cradled auto rifle and puts the barrel over his shoulder. He slowly casts a cautious eye in every direction and sniffs the air. The faint smell of spent gunpowder hints on the breeze and he motions them onward.

"C'mon, let's keep moving."

The morning rays of sunshine rise over the far tree line and the three fugitives move at a quickening pace, across the wide expanse of grasslands. After covering a distance, they halt their travel and pause for a break not far from a pair of flat-top, umbrella formed acacia trees. Several birds chatter and take flight from the far spreading canopy. The remainder of the idle flock observes the visitors in the open savannah.

To escape the midday sun, Mogambo ushers them to the shade of the wide reaching branches and lets the winged fowl above settle before he tilts his ear to the wind. The faint crack of gunshots can still be heard on the infrequent breeze and Roosevelt tries to listen as her shoulders repeatedly rise and fall to fill her lungs. The slight thumping sounds carried in the wind linger then cease and Tusk looks to Mogambo before giving a questioning swirl of his finger in the air.

"Is he headed this way?"

Mogambo turns to the horizon in the direction from which they just came and lifts his chin to the sky.

"Coming now."

Tusk tosses the auto rifle aside and begins to gather up some dry grass and sticks. He pulls a flint and steel from his shirt pocket and begins striking it in the nest of dry tinder. Roosevelt wipes the stream of sweat from her forehead and watches him, confused.

"What are you doing now? This doesn't seem the time or place for a cookout."

Tusk glances up at her then confirms a nod to Mogambo.

"Keep us covered with that rifle."

Mogambo grabs up the discarded auto rifle and scans their vacant surroundings. Amid Tusk's cupped fingers, a jumping spark grabs hold of the dry grass and starts a small flame which he gently whispers a steady breath of air into. The flame bursts brighter as Tusk blows a constant draft and he adds a small branch to the pile before fanning it with his hand.

"Signal fire."

Roosevelt stands, looking skeptical.

"You're signaling them back to us?"

"Just the chopper."

"So you can shoot it down again?"

The small fire grows in size and Tusk heaps larger sticks and handfuls of grass over the flames.

"Not sure who was operating the gun up there, but I'm pretty sure it was Butch behind the controls of that whirlybird."

"You mean he might be able to pick us up?"

"If he can find us ...."

Mogambo turns to look at Tusk then back to the sky.

"If Mister Butch is flying, I choose to walk."

Turning her gaze up to the sky, Roosevelt smiles at Tusk with reluctant approval and begins to gather more branches for the signal fire.

"Was this your plan all along?"

Tusk looks sideways at her with a widening grin.

"It is now."

XXVIII

A confined brushfire burns on the wide expanse of African grassy plain. The flames jump higher with the added branches and Tusk tosses some fresh groundcover onto the conflagration. The growing signal fire crackles and sizzles while sending up a shaft of thick smoke that forms a pluming, grey cloud.

Tusk stands and looks to the pair of trees nearby and a larger stand of foliage just beyond the open clearing. He motions to the thicker area of vegetation as he drags another broken tree limb over the fire.

"That's a good place to hide a while if we happen to attract the wrong kind of attention."

In the shade, Roosevelt watches the mound of greenery catch fire and lets her eyes travel skyward with the observable column of rising smoke.

"We will draw everyone in the area, I assume?"

Africa Tusk

"As long as the chopper is the first to arrive and we get clear of here, it doesn't really matter."

"What about containing the fire?"

"Range fires happen all the time, the grass will burn or it won't. Come on, let's go."

Tusk kicks another branch into the curling flames and escorts Roosevelt away toward the shelter of brush. The thick signal smoke wafts through the umbrella-top acacias and the winged fowl take flight. The fire crackles and burns behind as Mogambo follows cautiously with the rifle stock pressed at his shoulder.

The three figures move toward the patch of leafy cover and the distinct staccato sound of an aircraft with an impaired engine is heard, approaching from afar. Across the open clearing, the broken helicopter sounds get louder and Tusk grabs Roosevelt's arm to rush her to the concealment of the underbrush. They both turn, watching to the sky for the incoming chopper.

At the edge of the timberline, Mogambo holds the automatic rifle, sighted along his cheek while watching skyward. The signal fire near the isolated twin trees continues to roll smoke to the heavens as Tusk and Roosevelt hide themselves in the concealing thicket. Stifled in the dense underbrush, the three fugitives sweat profusely in the humid air.

They watch the horizon and observe as the damaged, smoke-trailing helicopter careens across the sky and smashes into the tops of the two large acacia trees near the signal fire. In a whirl of broken branches, rotor blades and smoldering engine, the sleek black military chopper tumbles through the limbs and hangs entangled midway down the tree's canopy. Tusk and Mogambo glance to each other in dismay as the aircraft settles and creaks to a standstill, a strange display of machinery intertwined with nature.

Roosevelt snorts in a disparaging tone lacking any hint of surprise at the unfortunate situation.

"There goes another first-rate rescue."

Tusk turns to stare across his shoulder at her.

"I'm beginning to think you're the jinx."

"How so, when you're the one who keeps screwing it up?"

His mouth agape, Tusk is about to tell her off when Mogambo nudges him and gestures in the direction of the crashed helicopter.

The side cargo door creaks ajar and one of Tusk's safari crewmen lowers his body to a supporting limb. The man gingerly climbs through the tree and gives a jostle on the airframe to check its stability in the branches. After peering inside through the front windscreen, the native man reaches out and opens the pilot side door.

Instantly a large framed body tumbles out and bounces off several tree boughs before crashing to the ground with a groaning thud. Tusk turns to glance at Roosevelt again and she shakes her head judgmental.

"Is that our fearless rescuer and associate?"

The safari hunter raises an eyebrow as he nods his affirmation of the helicopter pilot's identity.

"Ol' Butch isn't one to miss out on the action."

Below the tangled crash site, the signal fire still crackles and pops, sending wafts of smoke skyward.

Africa Tusk

Tusk and Mogambo rush across the clearing to Butch's motionless form and roll him over gently. The hulking mess of khaki safari garb that fell from above takes a deep breath and coughs.

Tusk holds Butch's head and shoulders off the ground and taps his whiskered cheek with his fingertips.

"You still alive pard?"

Butch opens his eyes and pauses before heaving a shrug.

"Well, I guess this surely ain't heaven if you're here to greet me."

"Anything broke from your fall?"

"Fall? Hell, I was motioning for that dunderhead not to open that door. Damn near broke my neck after a fine treetop landing!"

He cracks a smile as he looks up at the native crewman slowly descending his way through the branches.

The helicopter hangs precariously with the nose pointed downward in a twisted mess of broken limbs. Butch lets his amused gaze hover over to Tusk.

"I don't think that whirlybird has anymore flight time left in 'er."

Tusk grins and nods.

"Nice landing, Ace."

"How about that timing of my rescue?"

Roosevelt steps forward and peers down at Butch.

"The first part was good … you have to work on the ending."

Tusk and Mogambo help Butch gather his feet under him as the other safari crewman drops from the tree the remaining distance to the ground. The native gives a salute to Tusk and stands alongside Mogambo.

Butch dusts off his clothing and feels around his body for broken parts then smiles at Roosevelt.

"Just getting to the good part, Missy."

She stands poised before him and stares up to the crashed helicopter looming in the twin trees above.

"Are you saying you deliberately meant to smash our only hope of escape into the canopy of a tree?"
Butch gawks at her then over at Tusk and Mogambo.

"Escape … hell, what's she talking about?"
Tusk shrugs, looking away to survey the adjacent area.

"She was under the impression we were helpless prisoners about to be killed."

A wave of heat swirls past as the waning signal fire responds to the irregular breeze. Roosevelt takes a wider stance as she stares inquisitively at Tusk.

"Am I missing something here, Mister Kalispell?"
Separating himself from the group, Mogambo listens to the sounds in the wind and motions with the auto-rifle.

"Bwana, we must be gone now."

Tusk nods, smirks at Roosevelt and follows off after Mogambo. Becoming exasperated, the lady doctor looks at the departing safari party and the empty landscape before them.

"Where are we headed now and will someone please tell me what's going on?"
Butch steps forward to put his arm across her shoulder. His hot breath invades her senses as he whispers the planned secret close at her cheek.

"We got the ol' boy's jeep loaded with all your high tech equipment a few ticks south of here."

Africa Tusk

Shocked at the news and unexpected strategy, Roosevelt lets herself be escorted along by Butch. They follow behind Tusk and Mogambo as they travel away from the signal fire. After thinking on the suggested scheme, she hesitates and looks at Butch curiously.

"You have all my gear? Everything?"

"As far as we can tell we do. It was a bit confusing puttin' it all together."

"What are we planning to do?"

Butch turns to the native crewman who follows behind and rattles off several commands in the Bantu dialect. Tusk halts, turns around and adds to the exchange, looks at Roosevelt then continues with a softened change of tone. Butch shrugs and Tusk nods his consent. The native crewman looks to the sun's position in the sky to get his bearings then lopes off toward the eastern horizon.

Roosevelt stands confused by the unintelligible provincial dialect of the terse conversation.

"What's happening? Where's that man going?" Tusk waves toward the lady doctor and ushers her in the direction of Mogambo's lead.

"We're not getting out of here, we're going back." Standing idle, Roosevelt can't believe what she's hearing.

"Are you all insane?"

Butch gives a hearty chuckle as he moves past her.

"Did you not see my treetop canopy landing?"

Tusk observes Roosevelt's reluctant reaction and stands with a changed, deadly serious demeanor.

"We're going to use that equipment of yours to clean out what's left of Hang and his ivory operation."

The professional hunter and lady doctor watch as Butch hustles to catch up with Mogambo who stands, waiting patiently. The safari man takes the automatic rifle from the gun bearer and turns the weapon upward toward the helicopter still snarled in the trees.

Taking aim, Butch squeezes off a few short bursts of gunfire and the fuel tanks are pierced. A steady stream of petroleum begins to leak from the perforated holes and puddle on the dry ground. Grabbing up a burning stick from the signal fire, Butch tosses it through the air to land in the petrol-soaked grasses beneath.

The flammables quickly ignite, leap into the tree canopy and cause the military helicopter to explode in a spectacular ball of fire. Roosevelt staggers back from the flames and nearly lands in Tusk's arms.

"Was that really necessary?"

Butch nods, satisfied, and hands Mogambo back the rifle. He does a short dancing jig followed by an exaggerated bow toward the observers with a grinning expression.

"It's the little pleasures in life that make it all worthwhile."

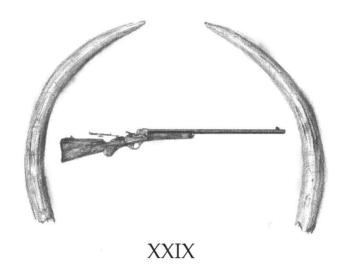

XXIX

The wide expanse of untamed wilderness is strangely quiet and the once teeming abundance of wildlife seems to have disappeared. Mogambo leads the small group of non-native fugitives to the hidden location. Still in sight range, far behind Butch at the rear, the billowing smoke from the destroyed helicopter can still be seen sending dark plumes skyward.

The group comes upon a patch of tall heavy brush and Mogambo quickly enters and weaves through the clinging brambles. Roosevelt peers back a moment then ducks into the brushwood to keep pace with Tusk and the others. She stays at Tusk's boot heels, pushing branches aside and ducking the recoiling limbs.

"Tell me again, so I don't misunderstand … what was the point of exploding the helicopter?"

"It sends a message."

She sighs sarcastically.

"Meaning what? That we didn't quite escape successfully?"

"That's a part of it."

Tusk swipes at the tall brush, hustling to keep pace with Mogambo and break trail for those following. Glancing over his shoulder, he makes sure Roosevelt is staying close as he stomps a path for her.

"In a few hours, when they look over the burnt wreckage, they won't find any of our bodies and that will infuriate them even more."

The lady doctor shields her face from razor sharp thorns and blades of grass as they swish past.

"I don't think you really have to try to upset anyone. They already don't like you."

Tusk resumes the quick foot pace through the thick scrub and turns with a serious look as he continues on.

"The only way to get to these poachers is to hit them hard in the pocketbook. Take away the profit or take away their resources."

"They murder thousands of elephants, so you blow up their helicopter?"

"Did you take notice how quick they had that thing in the air after I shot it down last time? What was it a day or so? It won't be flying again soon this time."

Roosevelt pushes a branch from her path and jogs to keep up with the strides of Tusk and Mogambo ahead.

"But, won't it lead them right to us?"

"We have only a few hours before they track us."

"And, how do you know that?"

Africa Tusk

"That's about how long it would take me. Logan is just as capable and has a crew of scouts. We could possibly have less time as he probably has a cracked jaw for extra motivation on the hunt."

The group emerges from the thick underbrush to another small clearing. Mogambo increases their pace forward at an easy trot and the others follow in step. Roosevelt pushes the sweat-matted hair back on her forehead as she runs behind, trying to speak between gasps of breath.

"So, the plan is to get at my anti-poaching technology, which is assembled on your jeep, then set up an ambush for them?"

Tusk tugs his hat down and turns to look at her.

"Only a small contingent will be sent after us. They still have that herd of tuskers to harvest."

Roosevelt's pace falters and she tries to catch a lungful while thinking of the herd's imminent peril.

"Really?"

"That's how I figure it."

Roosevelt redoubles her pace to catch up next to Tusk.

"They'll still kill them after all that's happened?"

"They won't whimper home to lick any wounds."

"But, haven't they lost enough?"

Sweat running down under his hat brim, Tusk swipes it aside and blows the drips from the tip of his nose.

"To them it's just a business expense."

"Just the injured men would surely cost them?"

"Yeah … and the price of ivory goes up."

Roosevelt jogs beside Tusk and utters between breaths.

"What about your man you sent off?

Eric H. Heisner

Tusk mops a stream of sweat that drips along his temple and adjusts his broad brim hat as he tosses a mischievous smirk toward her.

"That was plan B or possibly C."

"Which is?"

"What's gonna happen if all hell breaks loose."

Roosevelt falters her step trying to keep up and watches the men ahead of her jogging away. Butch comes up behind and ushers her along as she mutters aloud.

"Plan B or C? Hasn't everything all gone to piss 'nd shit already?"

Mogambo leads with Tusk silently following behind and Butch and Roosevelt bringing up the rear. Besides the column of smoke, the wide sprawling scope of the African savannah stretches to the horizon all around. The sight of foraging wildlife returns and the landscape seem unspoiled and devoid of the negative colonizing effects of human greed.

A soft breeze wavers through the tall grasses that dip into a secluded valley. Mogambo travels ahead of the small party toward another thicket of vegetation and stops at a large pile of intertwined, arranged brushwood. The native scout turns back to the group and flashes a wide grin before pulling branches from the stack. Tusk whistles softly and connects his gaze with Butch.

"My jeep is under there?"

"Somewhere's ... If we never came along, it would be lost to civilization."

Hands on his broad hips, Butch beams as he assesses the carefully amassed and woven brush.

Africa Tusk

"When I caught up with him, he was thinkin' of just drivin' the thing straight to ya."

Tusk and Butch move in to lend a hand and start pulling the carefully placed camouflage away to reveal a hint of the jeep beneath. Tusk pitches a leafy branch aside and peers inside the jumbled pile.

"He can really hide a vehicle."

Sweat markings on her khaki blouse, Roosevelt stands back and watches. Twisted sections of branches are tossed away as the men work in the midday heat. She observes attentively as the anti-poaching weapon mounted on the open-top jeep is slowly unveiled.

A small assembly of armed tribesmen pauses, looking up at the black smoke that continues to climb skyward from the smoldering, tree-bound chopper. Stepping forward, the dark steely gaze of Peter Logan lets nothing escape his keen observation as he stands before the hunting party. He drops to a knee and picks up an empty shell casing from an automatic rifle. A short sniff of the brass cartridge tells him what he already knows and he looks from the leaving trail to the single tread of slightly trampled grass leading away.

Without uttering a word, he rises to his full height and shrewdly stares around in a final survey of the area. He turns to the tribesmen who stand ready with automatic weapons slung across sinewy shoulders. Waving a commanding gesture he assigns a man to the single departing foot trail and ushers the rest to follow in the continued hunt for their human quarry.

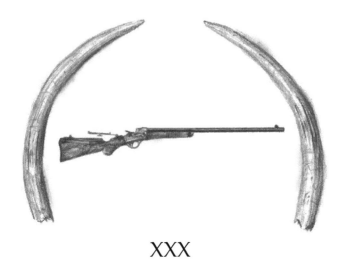

XXX

The final limbs of camouflage are pulled from the top-less Jeep Willys, scraping across the matte paint exterior. A trace of nervous perspiration makes its way down her temple and Roosevelt apprehensively steps forward to inspect the sought-after experimental weapon. Tusk kicks a stray branch away and steps alongside her to observe the lethal miscreation assembled in his jeep.

"Everything is there, I assume?"

Roosevelt is startled from her personal musings as Tusk reaches into the vehicle and hands over her laptop computer.

"Seems to be."

"Well, make sure of it. We need to get it going." Roosevelt looks at Tusk questioningly.

"Right now?"

Africa Tusk

"The sooner the better, I'd say. We have a gang of mercenary cutthroats on our back trail and a herd of elephants that is being set up for slaughter as we speak." She stares at the weapon and brushes leaves and thorny twigs from the surface of her computer. Her eyes scan the assembly of equipment as she powers up the keypad.

"It's just that this thing can take some time."

"Well, get to it ..."

Perpetually even-keeled, Tusk seems at the threshold of a swelling temper. He sweeps his hand across the driver's seat to clear it of brush debris and shakes his head as he watches the electronic weapon power up. His obvious aversion to the boundless possibilities of the overseeing drone technology is expressed through the tone of his terse reply.

"You sure had it set up in a jiffy surveilling over me the other day. How is this any different?"

"That was just a test run."

"Well this is a life or death run, so make it work." Roosevelt and glares at Tusk across the jeep.

"Don't pressure me!"

Trying to control his agitation, Tusk wags a finger at Roosevelt and clenches his jaw.

"We need that thing up in the air immediately if not sooner and to get moving away from here, now!" The lady doctor murmurs a few choice obscenities toward Tusk and returns her attention to the electronics before her. The professional hunter shakes his head, checks the ignition key in the jeep and steps away to where Butch and Mogambo wait. Butch draws a small cigar from his pocket and tosses it between his teeth.

"How long will it take her?"

Tusk takes a deep calming breath and tries to quell his feelings of urgency.

"She said she's working on it."

Butch lights the cigar, eyes turned upward at Tusk.

"We're going to drive that rocket thing attached to yer jeep while the unit is flying around up there?"

Mogambo stands expressionless while Butch blows out a puff of smoke and pinches a loose bit of tobacco from his lip. A bemused smirk hints at the edges of Tusk's mouth as he looks over the unsightly high-tech contraption mounted on his cherished vehicle.

"Since when are you one to heed any sort of cautionary measures? Puttering around with a once tested computer-controlled field gun that can decimate distant targets seems right up your alley."

"I was just worried about your jeep."

"Good, you can drive."

Butch chokes on an accidental lungful of inhaled smoke and takes the small cheroot from his teeth.

"Did that sound to you like me volunteering?"

"Well, Mogambo can drive then."

A spark of excitement dances in the native tracker's eyes and the burly safari man leans over toward Tusk and lowers his voice.

"Hell, he's a good chap 'nd all, but a damn worse driver than you on an off-day."

Tusk pats Butch on the shoulder and smiles.

"Hey, it's something to do."

Butch ashes his cigar and chomps it between his teeth.

"It'll keep me awake at least."

Africa Tusk

They both turn their attention to Roosevelt as the drone powers up with a loud buzzing hum. Sounding like an oversized mosquito, the eight miniature props lift the gyro computer and camera a few feet into the air. With laptop in hand, Roosevelt maneuvers the drone up and down in a tight circular maneuver then lands it again just behind the jeep before looking over at Tusk with a nod.

"All set to go up. We can launch it anytime."
Tusk turns to Butch and Mogambo and gives a twirling motion of his hand at the wrist.

"Okay then, let's move out!"

The wilderness of east-central Africa spreads out endlessly along the horizon as the jeep tears along the terrain with a trail of dust rising from its path. Butch steers with Mogambo belted into the passenger seat alongside him. In the back, Tusk sits amongst the piles of equipment with Roosevelt and hangs onto the side rail to keep from bouncing out. She attempts to tinker with the electronics on the big gun and is obviously frustrated by trying to steady her hand in the moving vehicle.

Tusk peers around the towering contraption positioned between them as she works and grunts.

"I thought you said this thing was ready to go?"
Her eyes peer up at him with an annoyed intensity.

"The drone is working fine. This weapon needs some adjustment before it will target properly. Doing it in the back of this bounce-house isn't the ideal setting."

"It's not functional then?"

"Not quite yet."

"So as it stands, we could see everything from the drone but may not be able to do a damn thing about it?" Roosevelt glares at Tusk and gives him a roll of her eyes as she resumes her unsteady adjustments.

"I'm working on it."

They both grasp for a firm handhold as the jeep bounces and swerves around a cratered sinkhole. Butch steers to a clearing and jams the vehicle in neutral. The adept driver reaches into his breast pocket and draws out another small ragged cigarillo.

"This is it. We're about a kilometer from where that tusker herd was at the yonder watering hole."

Tusk swings his body over the side and drops his booted feet to the ground. He turns to Roosevelt as she continues to make alterations on the target mechanism.

"All ready with that thing yet?"

Roosevelt continues her technical work and taps out a few commands on the keyboard.

"Like I said, the drone is fine, but I need to do some fine tuning of the weapon."

Butch looks over his shoulder from the driver's seat.

"Does that mean it won't shoot?"

In a huff, Roosevelt grimaces at Tusk then calms herself as she turns to Butch. In her most composed professional manner she replies.

"The weapon will shoot perfectly on command, but it's important to know exactly *where* it will shoot." Butch ponders a short moment and nods.

"Agreed."

The lap belt clicks off and Mogambo climbs out from the passenger seat. He eyeballs the bizarre, mysterious weapon in the back of the jeep before taking an automatic rifle over to a nearby tree and shimmying up as a lookout. Butch watches the native scout climb the branches and perch himself a safe distance away.

"Ol' Mogambo there has the right idea, getting far away from this thing, I think."

Tusk moves around the jeep, slides his big bore hunting rifle out of the leather scabbard on the side and sets it near the driver's door. He reaches behind the seat, pulls out a cartridge belt full of .45-70 ammunition and buckles it on. Positioned opposite the vehicle from Roosevelt, he heaves the heavy rifle to the crook of his arm as she continues to work on the computer.

"Do what you can to get that thing operating."
She looks up from the keypad questioningly.

"Where are you going?"

The safari hunter hangs a set of distance glasses around his neck and gives the antique Remington long-gun a familiar pat before he begins to hike off toward the direction of the elephants.

"I'm going to head over there and save what I can of that herd the old-fashioned way."

"You're kidding, I nearly have this ready!"
Striding away, Tusk raises a hand with a curt goodbye wave. Roosevelt begins to protest and Butch comes up beside her and puts his hand gently to her shoulder.

"Let 'em go, Doc. There's nothing worse for the tortured mind than standing around waiting. He needs to be doing something and you don't need him breathing down your neck."

She shakes her head with a calming sigh and gives Butch's hand a friendly pat before resuming her skilled tinkering on the computer pad.

"You're right, I need to focus on the task at hand. Let him go and do whatever he's going to do anyway." The burly companion leans back on the fender of the jeep and watches Tusk disappear into the faraway brush.

"You just get that thing working like before … except of course, there's no helicopter this time."

"Only more armed poachers to contend with."

"More'n just a few … Remember, they're coming up behind as well as in front of us now." Roosevelt looks aside at Butch then up to the tree where Mogambo sits watchful and senses their apprehension.

"Yeah, no pressure."

XXXI

The Willys Jeep sits at the edge of the grazed clearing with Mogambo perched in a nearby tree, watching the far horizon. Butch paces impatiently like an expectant new father as Roosevelt works on the GPS coding for the anti-poaching weapon. He halts in his tracks, listens to the faint pop of gunfire away in the distance, turns on his heel and struts back toward the jeep.

"Not to rush you darlin', but those aren't fire-crackers ya hear cracklin' o'er yonder."
She shakes her head to fend off any distraction and resumes tapping away at the electronic formulations.

"You should have just gone along with him if you're going to nag at me too?"
A heavy leather boot perches on the driver's door cutaway and the vehicle leans down in Butch's direction.

He crosses his arms over his raised knee and taps his fingers on the big steel ring of a steering wheel.

"Who would drive this thing?"

Roosevelt's typing fingers pause and she looks at Butch.

"Drive it?"

"That's part of the, *we need to keep moving so they don't catch us* plan, Missy."

"You're kidding?"

"Afraid not … I thought you understood that plain 'nough? We can't stay here any longer. Logan and his boys will most likely be tracking near to us soon."

Showing an expression of doubt, Roosevelt looks at the complex anti-poaching cannon setup in the back of the all-terrain vehicle. Her uncertain gaze travels to the drone device resting on the folded down windscreen.

"We can't drive this thing and shoot it too."

"Why the hell not?"

"It hasn't been tested."

Butch scratches the whiskers on his chin and half-grins.

"Not yet …"

From the tree canopy, Mogambo whistles down a shrill warning call. Butch stands, looks around and returns the high-pitched signal while Mogambo quickly descends the lookout position. Roosevelt watches as the native scout with the rifle hustles toward the ground and Butch slides into the driver's chair, adjusting the positioning of the pistol holstered at his side. Butch turns back to her and waves a harried salute.

"There's no time like the present, Doc."

"You're kidding?"

"You keep saying that, but we haven't come up short and disappointed you yet."

"How about the helicopter and failed rescues?"

"You're rescued now ain't ya?"

Roosevelt puts the laptop computer aside and slides down into a seated position at the back of the jeep where she won't bounce out. Butch looks ahead at the drone setup on the flattop hood and turns the ignition key on the jeep. The engine roars to life and Roosevelt hollers forward to Butch in the driver's seat.

"You think we can drive around in this spring-board and shoot this weapon with any sort of accuracy?"

Mogambo jogs over and leaps into the passenger chair. He tucks the rifle at his side and buckles on the lap safety belt. Butch jams his foot on the clutch pedal and looks back at Roosevelt.

"It's time to launch that thing. Do your best since we ain't got a choice 'bout it. They're a comin' now."

Roosevelt shakes her head with concern as she powers up the small propellers on the drone. The unit rocks lightly as the multiple engines hum on the hood of the vibrating jeep. Mogambo pushes back into his chair, wide-eyed and glances beside to the driver's seat. Butch turns and looks behind at Roosevelt with a tense grin while the eight spinning props buzz the air about a meter from his face.

"Are those little buggers sharp?"

"Like a food processor."

The drone begins to drift upward while Butch and Mogambo lean toward the jeep's cutaway door openings, preparing for a quick exit. The native tracker puts his hand to the seat harness buckle, ready to release it and bail out at a moment's notice. In the rear position, Roosevelt swipes her finger over a touch pad and the hovering drone tilts and rises.

"Don't worry I can fly this thing in my sleep."

Butch lets out a stifled breath and stares ahead of the vehicle while the airborne drone moves forward and rises into the sky. He peers over his shoulder and smiles.

"Great, but can you fly it from the back of a bouncing jeep while under hostile gunfire?"

"As I said, it hasn't been tested."

He grinds the shifter into gear and gooses the gas line.

"Are you ready for its first run?"

Roosevelt steers the drone higher up into the cloudless sky and speaks just as the jeep begins to roll forward.

"Butch…"

"Yeah, kid?"

"What will we do when we lock in on a target?"

There is a sense of looming culpability as the trio from vastly different circumstances face an imminent decision. Roosevelt barely gets the words out when Butch lets off the clutch and hammers on the gas pedal. They tear off across the clearing and Butch hollers back.

"Duck, I guess."

The narrow axle jeep laden with the advanced technology, anti-poaching cannon aboard bounces along the rough terrain. Dust rolls up from the wheel wells as Roosevelt attempts to enter coding information into her laptop. She tilts her screen to reduce the glare and wipes a film of dust from the upper portion of the monitor.

Africa Tusk

The live-feed video surveillance clearly shows the aerial perspective of their previous location.

Roosevelt leans forward and taps Butch on the shoulder. He stretches back to look at the screen while still driving and she points to an object on the monitor.

"Do you see that?"

"What is it?"

A small truck appears on the scene along with several native men afoot and the side door opens to a figure stepping out to inspect the recent trail. Roosevelt points at the miniature human forms on her laptop monitor.

"It's the group of men who are tracking us."

Butch faces forward again and continues to drive the jeep at a rapid but controlled speed.

"Looks like a good time to test this thing."

"Really?"

"No time to get squeamish honey!"

Roosevelt looks to the faceless figures on the screen of her monitor and feels a guilty pang of conscience.

"But they're just …"

The jeep swerves and Butch gazes back at the lady doctor with a grave expression.

"They're just nothing at all, except on the hunt and looking for blood. That they don't have a victim in their sights doesn't make them any less murderous."

Butch turns forward, continuing to steer, and speaks loudly over his shoulder at her.

"Think about what they did yesterday or what they will do tomorrow after they execute us."

Roosevelt takes a deep calming breath, shifts the drone perspective higher and types in the arming codes.

The large space-age cannon mounted on the jeep hums to life, pivots and points skyward. She whispers faintly.

"It's almost ready."

While navigating the jeep, Butch peers over his seatback at the computer visuals as small grey targeting crosshairs waver over the unsuspecting figures around the stationary truck. Butch takes a quick look ahead then back at Roosevelt skeptical.

"What's it gonna take to shoot it?"

Bracing her knee to the back of the forward seat, she tries to hold the laptop steady.

"The weapon signal is having a hard time locking the objectives with your inconsistent driving."

Butch turns forward and tries to steady the jeep on the open terrain.

"Yes, Miss Daisy!"

Positioning her finger over the touch pad, the computer flashes red warning symbols on the selected targets. Roosevelt looks up at Butch and Mogambo.

"It's locked on all targets."

A white knuckled grip on the steering wheel, Butch sits low in the seat and Mogambo puts his hands over his dark scalp for cover. Butch glances back and nods the go-ahead to Roosevelt.

"Alright, do it."

Roosevelt hesitates, looks forward at Butch and shakes her head with a morbid reluctance.

"I don't think I can execute these people."

"You do it, or they will do the same to us!"

She stares at the featureless human targets on the impersonal computer display and feels a deep sense of agony.

Africa Tusk

The small figures holding guns move around and congregate near the idle military truck like fictitious characters in a teenage video game.

The snapping clap of gunfire from faraway seems suddenly nearer as they drive closer to the condemned elephant herd. The horrific visual of an animal with its face removed by a chain-saw, flashes into Roosevelt's thoughts and clouds her vision. Butch tries to hold the jeep steady and calls back over his shoulder.

"Now or never Honey, we're almost to the herd site. We'll have another tough job ahead of us there."

Sick feelings well up at the pit of her stomach as Roosevelt ruminates on the plight of the endangered creatures. She concentrates on her computer screen, tentatively taps the 'target engage' icon and the anti-poaching cannon rattles then hums. Before the three in the jeep can react, blazing bolts of lighted fire shoot from the cannon in rapid succession.

Butch swerves to a stop and puts an arm over the short seatback to watch the video screen in Roosevelt's lap. They observe as the human targets on the computer monitor are each methodically hit and tossed aside like animated miniatures. The poacher truck pulls forward, swerves and jacks hard to the side as the driver is blasted into his seat from the aerial projectile coming through the windshield.

Nauseated, Roosevelt closes the folding laptop device and tries to control her overwhelming emotions. Butch remains stone-faced, sighs and turns forward to shift the jeep back into gear. He murmurs over his slumped shoulder toward Roosevelt.

"Don't close it down yet, Doctor … we still have a lot of work ahead of us."

A streaming tear rolls down Roosevelt's cheek and she quickly swipes it away and looks up at Butch.

"Fine, let's go away from here and get to it."
Butch nods understandingly and stares ahead. The jeep's rear wheels spin out and the open-toped, armed vehicle tears off in a cloud of dirt toward the deathly crackle of gunshots in the near distance.

XXXII

The earsplitting trumpet of injured elephants puts a gut-wrenching sense of panic into the air. The pachyderm family gathers around a fallen bull elephant as it wails from inflicted gunshot wounds. Attempting to shelter their fallen brethren, some animals angrily face off to the approaching machine gun toting poachers while others scatter to protect the young.

Sprays of hot lead projectiles shot from automatic military rifles thud and bounce off the thick, wrinkled hides of the majestic beasts. Not far away, Tusk watches the appalling violence through a pair of field glasses. He quickly scans the targeted range and does a mental count of the aggressive poachers setting up a loose perimeter to contain the herd with rifle fire.

"You damn bastards ..."

Eyes squinted hard; Tusk puts his long range, Remington Rolling Block rifle to his shoulder. He cocks back the hammer and draws a bead on one of the poachers firing an AK-47 auto rifle. Trumpeting cries from the injured animals pulse through Tusk's being as he takes a holding breath and squeezes the trigger.

An emotional ache grips at his chest several beats until the murderous ivory poacher catches the large caliber bullet in the chest. The assassinated gunman spins to the ground and the firing rifle is tossed aside. The machine gun sputters the remainder of the clip as it hits the dirt, sending friendly fire into the harvest crew.

"That'll hurt in the morning ..."

Tusk quickly reloads a fresh cartridge and takes aim again. He squeezes off another shot and the human target slams against a truck door with a gaping shoulder wound. The injured crewman rolls away and ducks down in hiding. Tusk ejects the hot brass shell casing and slams in another finger-sized round as he curses under his breath.

"Shit ... he's gonna get away."

He puts the field glasses to his face and observes as the gun-toting predators get on the radio and begin to retreat to the relative safety of the vehicles. Lowering the binoculars, he cocks back the hammer, shoulders the rifle and sights the long gun on one of the truck's grill emblems. The sporadic sound of machine gun fire against the elephant herd continues as the illegal ivory hunters shoot from the cover of parked vehicles.

With several men aboard, the military style truck in the distance starts up and begins to drive forward.

Africa Tusk

Tusk takes the shot and after several long seconds, the vehicle rolls ahead with a spout of steam squirting out from the hole in the grill. The truck engine roars from an influx of gas which is followed shortly by a muffled grinding clang as the engine seizes. Drawing another cartridge from his ammunition belt, Tusk reloads as the poachers position themselves around the disabled vehicle and send scattered rounds of gunfire in his general direction.

Over a kilometer away on the periphery of the hunt, Su Long Hang sits in his dark windowed SUV and monitors the chatter on the handheld radio. His bleak features flush with rage as he slaps his hand down on the luxury leather seat.

"Imbeciles … just shoot him already!"

Hang pulls the passenger handle and kicks at the lower panel to swing the door ajar. He steps out and marches to the other transport vehicles, yelling at the native crew chief in command.

"Arm every man available, get in your trucks and circle around that positon. Flush him out and waste no time in executing him. I want his head on a platter!"

The tall, dark man nods hurriedly and hustles to one of the three waiting trucks. He jabbers into a radio receiver clipped to the shoulder epaulet on his shirt and the trucks all roar to life. Men from camp with rifles rush to the vehicles and cling to the running boards as the mercenary transports roll out for the manhunt.

The afternoon sun shines down hot as Tusk crouches low in the tall, thick grass. He watches closely as the other teams of ivory poachers pull back from the hunt and begin to circle on his flank. The distress calls from injured elephants broadcast across the savannah and Tusk does a quick assessment of the depleted ammunition supply on his belt.

"Hmm … I may have gotten myself into it now."

Tusk shoulders his rifle and throws a shot at one of the moving trucks partially obscured through a patch of umbrella topped trees. The heavy round smashes through the driver's side door and the vehicle rolls to a stop, still idling. His back up against a thorny acacia tree, Tusk looks to his flank and can faintly make out concealed figures moving through the heavy brush. He spots another set of trucks coming on and nods with a somber realization.

"Well, this might be it … *Tusk's last stand*."

Backed against the spikey vegetation, Tusk sits with his rifle rested on his knee, watching for any movement coming toward him. Sweating and waiting patiently in the heat, he observes as distant grasses are slowly pushed aside. He puts his cheek to the rifle stock and pulls the trigger to fire into the center of the effort. A yelping grunt rolls over in the bush followed by the low wail of a wounded man.

Dropping down on an elbow to reload and position on the ground, Tusk eases the field glasses to his face and assesses his dangerous and slowly deteriorating position. Another set of military looking trucks roll up across the open field of conflict and a dozen armed men scatter to the brush. In the gentle breeze, Tusk can almost hear the muffled chatter on the radios between the wails of the injured elephants.

The late day sun begins to glisten golden on the tall grasses and long shadowed trees. The Willys Jeep revs and bounces across scenic landscape as Roosevelt sits in back next to the weapon, gripping a hold on her laptop computer while still trying to type adjustments to target the device. Butch sits deep in the driver's seat with both hands on the wheel as the loaded jeep skims across the grassy terrain.

He hollers behind over the roar of the engine and the scratching sounds of trail brush on metal side panels.

"How we doing back there?"

"It's going about as smoothly as you're driving." Butch turns forward and quickly swerves around a monument sized termite hill. The jeep bucks over a berm and Butch reaches back to grab hold of Roosevelt's knee to keep her inside the vehicle.

"We should be close. I'll find us some cover."

Roosevelt continues to work on her laptop, watching the aerial image from the perspective of the drone. The camera visuals seem to drift randomly and Roosevelt leans forward to holler over Butch's shoulder.

"I can't control any sort of steady targeting with you driving like you are."

Mogambo holds a death grip on the door frame to keep from bouncing out and smiles wide as Butch grimaces. He steers toward the scant shelter of some medium sized trees and turns the key to cut the engine.

The burdened jeep glides to a stop in the broken shade as Butch pulls his hands from the steering wheel and lays them across his lap.

"How's that for smooth?"

He scoots up on the backrest and leans over to take a look at the computer monitor in Roosevelt's lap.

"Any sign of them following us?"

Roosevelt looks up from the screen at him questioningly.

"Who's them?"

"Those men back there, who you blasted."

"Why would they follow us?"

The safari man meets her gaze and seems concerned.

"Well, you got a camera in the air so I thought you might get a final look-see if you got them all?"

A look of contempt crosses her features and she turns her attentions back to the computer monitor.

"No … I don't gloat over the victims."

Butch shakes his head dismissively.

"It ain't gloating honey when you're in the right."

He watches the bird's eye view of the drone video on the monitor and studies the landscape intently.

"Where's that at?"

Roosevelt raises the drone to get a wider perspective.

"It should be just to the west of here."

The drone footage remains stationary and Butch points at a sliver of movement and brief flashes of light.

"Over there is the watering hole."

Roosevelt gestures to another area on the video feed.

"The elephants are gathered here in this section."

The broad shouldered hunter kneels on the driver's chair and jabs his finger at the visuals on the computer screen.

"Check this out. I saw some gun flashes!"

The drone directs the camera over to the cluster of murdered elephants surrounding the downed bull near the watering hole. Roosevelt swipes the screen and zeros in on the perspective image with tears forming glassy across her eyes. Butch taps her hand and yells impatiently at her.

"No, no not that way … over here!"

The camera pans over to where he points and she zooms in on a lone holdout at the very center of a loose circling of trucks and armed men. Roosevelt shakes her head disbelievingly when she recognizes Tusk. The solitary figure with the single-shot rifle sits in the crossfire of an army of ivory-poaching mercenaries.

"Damn … he's like a magnet."

"Yeah, for shit-storms."

Roosevelt looks over at Butch with trepidation.

"I guess that's a subtle way to put it."

She expands the view of the wide lensed camera with a touch of the screen and they are able to see with less detail, the whole setup of poachers and vehicles moving in on Tusk's surrounded position. A short distance away, the massacred herd of elephants is strewn about the blood tinged watering hole. Butch climbs out of the jeep and stands over Roosevelt's shoulder at the rear side panel.

"Can you get him out of there?"

Her eyes remain focused on the drone flight and targeting controls as she shakes her head.

"Too spread out. I can only lock a few at a time."

Butch draws his sidearm and chambers a round.

"Better get to it then. At least make him a hole in their ranks for a chance to get away."
Butch holds his firearm at his side and studies the layout of advancing poachers. He taps her hand and gestures to a possible route of escape for Tusk.

"Take those men out first!

"Yes, yes, I'm trying ..."

Roosevelt swipes rapidly at her touchpad, types a few commands, and the drone's camera scans the attacking poacher's advance on the lone safari hunter. The bird's eye view of the dire situation sends up a sick feeling from the bottom of her gut. The lethal grey symbols of targeting crosshairs float across the screen until a single icon blinks red.

XXXIII

Beads of sweat stream down Tusk's flushed temples as he hunkers low in the grass, holding his rifle tight to his shoulder. The whistle of gunfire crisscrosses over him like the ripping of silk. With the army of mercenary poachers closing in, Tusk stays near to the ground and waits for an unsuspecting mark to enter his iron sights. He determines the source of gunshots coming from all directions and optimistically considers the prospect of the shooters injuring each other in the crossfire.

From above, a slight buzzing hum catches his attention and Tusk turns to cast his gaze into the afternoon sky. The dark outline of a drone hovers overhead as the fleeting whiz of bullets continues to zip through the grasses. Tusk shakes his head, crestfallen.

"Rescued twice in one week … they'll never let me live this down."

He eases the field glasses to his face and looks up at the hovering object, high above. Faintly, he can see the gimballed camera mount in the center of the ring of spinning propellers. The wide lens glistens as it rotates and scans the area then points straight down at him. He hooks a thumb over his shoulder and gestures to an intended route of escape. Suddenly, the binoculars are ripped from his hand as a bullet crashes past, splintering the frame into shards of glass and punctured metal.

Tusk winces at the jolting sting of his hand and looks back to see the movement of several forms in the grass raking the brush with hostile gunfire. He rolls to his back and eases the tip of his rifle muzzle up over the toe of his boot. Taking careful aim, Tusk squeezes off a shot causing the poacher standing at the middle of the group to reel in a backward somersault while his gun finishes its semi-auto round of fire.

Stray bullets spray over the heads of the other poachers in the lineup who quickly halt their progress and duck for cover. A hot brass casing is removed from the breech of the long range gun and Tusk pulls another from his belt, slamming it into the chamber.

"I guess the time to make my move is now or possibly never."

Reloaded, Tusk clutches his rifle to his chest, rolls over and clambers through the thick undergrowth and scrub. The rattling pop of machine gun fire continues across the tops of the waist-high grass as the khaki clad figure scrambles away.

Africa Tusk

At the jeep with the anti-poaching weapon mounted aboard, Butch stands behind Roosevelt as she zeros in on several targets. He grips his big mitt on her shoulder and points to the slightest movement on screen.

"There … he's moving, best make him a path."
Fingers flutter over the touchpad as she tries to quell her frustration with Butch clinging at her shoulder.

"This thing isn't built for evasive action or split-second tactical maneuvers."
The monitor screen lights up with targets locked and this time, Roosevelt doesn't hesitate to execute the command.

The burdened jeep rocks on its narrow, thick-knobbed tires as the anti-poaching cannon blasts several rounds into the air in rapid succession. Wide-eyed, Mogambo takes a cautious step back from the equipped vehicle and Butch whistles through his teeth as he watches the video feed, waiting for contact. He glances over at Mogambo and motions for him to check around.

"Mogambo, you best keep a lookout on our perimeter. We may be here for a spell."
Roosevelt turns away from the appalling sight on the monitor and looks to Butch with a sickened demeanor.

"How many more will we have to eliminate?"
"We need to clean house."

Thorns and thick razor edge, blades of grass slice at Tusk as he scrambles through the underbrush. He pulls his hat down hard and glimpses past his shoulder at one of the mercenary assailants raising a weapon to take aim. He swings his long barreled rifle around and shoots from the hip. The poacher squeezes a few rounds from his automatic rifle before the heavy lead bullet slug catches him in the high chest area. The gunshot inflicted body spins around with his arms flailing and rifle tumbling away.

The sound of the Remington's breech opening and an empty brass shell casing being discarded is followed by the *plunk* of a fresh cartridge slamming in. The barrage of shooting seems to pause a brief moment as Tusk jumps to his feet and starts running. Ahead in his path, several men rise from the bush with their military arsenal held at the ready. Tusk puts his loaded rifle to his shoulder and fires as he charges toward them.

As if by some dark witchcraft, the lineup of armed poachers is unceremoniously smashed to the ground by a slight incoming whistle and unforeseen force from above. Tusk continues dashing forward at a quickened pace and lowers his rifle as he reloads. He moves past the group of downed victims and gives a grateful wave skyward.

The sporadic rattle of continued machine gun fire from the battleground location of the cropped elephant herd makes the main poacher encampment nearby seem deathly idle. Su Long Hang's dark windowed Mercedes sits at the edge of the camp and the seething business-man paces a worn path in the trampled grass alongside. A handheld radio on the dashboard of the SUV, chatters excitedly and the Chinamen turns and glares at the small receiver with a mounting frustration.

Africa Tusk

Su Long Hang marches over past his waiting driver, grabs the handheld radio from the vehicle and spits angry venom into the receiver.

"Kill him! Kill him! Can't you kill him already?" The radio squawks quiet for a long pause and comes alive again with more chatter in native tongue. Su Long Hang tosses the radio into the driver's chest and shakes his head mystified.

"The man is like a damned ghost in the tall grass. I should have killed him easily when I had the chance."

Hang points at the radio in his henchman's hand and furiously sputters out his commands to be relayed.

"Tell them ... tell them to just turn back on the ivory harvest before the buzzards start to circle. We'll grab our reward so we can salvage this situation."
The short statured man faces the vacant camp and gazes at the sun's position as it crosses to the western horizon. He hollers past his shoulder to his man with the radio.

"Order the chain-saw crews into place."

With a determined step, Su Long Hang turns on his heels and marches back to the comforts of his vehicle. He climbs inside, draws out his phone and nestles into the soft leather seat as his driver secures the door behind him. The golden rays from afternoon sunlight shimmer forebodingly off dark-tinted windows as the sound of chainsaws sputtering to life erupts in the distance.

XXXIV

The warm afternoon air is heavy with the exhibition of death as Butch stands at Roosevelt's shoulder, watching the activity on the computer monitor. She readjusts the aerial perspective on the enemy positions as they appear to move away from pursuing the solitary hunter. Butch breathes down her neck and asks impatiently.

"What's going on?"

"They're pulling back."

He shades the monitor with his palm, shaking his head.

"Why would they do that?"

Roosevelt steers the drone camera away from Tusk's most recent position and follows the unified retreat. The remaining trucks and armed men circle around toward the watering hole and the flash of gunfire resumes in the direction of the downed elephant herd.

Roosevelt gets cold chills as the small flickers of light appear on the monitor screen.

"They're turning back on the herd."

Her fingers typing frantically on the keyboard, Roosevelt tries to lock in on a selection of targets. She stops suddenly when a shrill warning whistle is heard. The signal of danger puts Butch on instant alert and he scans around for Mogambo. He moves to the driver's side of the jeep and promptly catches a bullet in the arm that spins him against the forward panel and to the dirt.

Roosevelt ducks down, tosses her laptop into the front seat of the jeep and crawls around next to Butch.

"Are you shot?"

"Hell yeah, I am ... the bloody bastards!"

She peeks around the jeep bumper and spots Logan and two other men emerging from the trees at a running jog across the clearing toward them. Each man has his rifle raised and ready to shoot as they trot closer. She swallows the lump in her throat and gasps.

"It's Logan ..."

"No shit?"

Keeping her head low, Roosevelt sneaks a quick look around the vehicle at the mercenaries and judges their distance to the jeep.

"They'll be here in less than a minute. What do you want me to do?"

Butch winces as he draws his pistol across his chest.

"I'm gonna kill that sonovabitch."

She looks to the weaponized jeep and shakes her head.

"We have to keep this from the wrong hands."

"Take the jeep and get the hell out of here!"

Butch clenches his jaw and reaches out to grab hold of Roosevelt's arm with a firm squeeze.

"And don't argue with me ... just do it!"

Roosevelt looks down at the traces of blood smeared on Butch's hand from holding where the bullet entered his arm. The stern expression on the oversized safari hunter leaves no room for argument. She glances up to the anti-poaching weapon again then unties her neckerchief and wraps it around his wound.

"Take care of that arm."

Attempting to keep low, Roosevelt climbs into the driver's side and peers over at her laptop on the passenger seat. The computer screen blinks with the selected targets still locked flashing red, waiting for the final command. She reaches down, grabs up the electronic device and looks out the side cutaway of the jeep at Logan and his men still steadily approaching across the open grassland.

Paused in thought, she considers the time it would take to reselect targets when a fired bullet snaps into the side view mirror and tiny shards of glass spray across Roosevelt's lap. She peers up again to see Logan and his two men break into a faster pace that quickly covers the terrain between. A hand reaches in from the side of the jeep and slaps firmly on her leg. Butch hollers as he crawls on a knee and pushes away from the jeep.

"Go now, dammit!"

With a turn of the ignition key in the dash, the engine roars to life. Roosevelt jabs her foot on the clutch and looks to Butch with his pistol in hand ready to fight as soon as the protective cover of the jeep is removed.

Another glance over her shoulder at Logan and she turns the key off and releases the clutch. Butch sinks to his haunches and sputters in dismay.

"What the hell are you doing?"

The open laptop lifts from the passenger seat and Roosevelt steps from the vehicle and holds the device out in front of her assertively; ready to confront Logan. The mercenary hunter slows to a stroll and lowers the aim of his rifle. With his full attention on the female doctor he signals the other tribesmen to stay alongside him and do the same. Logan continues forward a few steps and smiles a creepy smirk.

"Hello there, Dearie. Miss me much?"

"I didn't miss you in the way you think."

At the reference to the termination of his men, Logan's demeanor turns malicious. His steely gaze wanders over to the experimental weapon mounted on the jeep then returns to the laptop computer in her grasp.

"What have you got there? Checking email?" Roosevelt raises the flashing monitor for effect and threateningly positions her hand over the glowing keys.

"If you don't leave us be, I'll give the command."

Logan motions for his crewmen to halt and he continues to walk closer. He raises his hands, holding the rifle, high in the air. Slowly narrowing the distance, Logan stands before Roosevelt as she nervously keeps her finger poised over the keypad. He tosses his scoped rifle aside and in a lightening quick flash of movement grabs the compact electronic device from her hands.

"You're gonna do what?"

Shocked and embarrassed, Roosevelt suddenly stands stripped of any leverage or power in negotiation. She timidly glances back at Butch as he climbs up to a leaning position against the opposite panel of the jeep. His grazed arm wound bleeding down his shirtsleeve, Butch still holds his pistol in hand and pointed in the general direction of Logan.

"Not so fast there, Logan ol' pal."

The mercenary hunter grips the laptop and raises the other open palm in a calming gesture toward Butch. The multiple target icons on the monitor screen flash red and Logan stares down, studying the video location and aiming information. The two armed tribesmen remain a few steps away with their rifles ready to put into action. Logan grunts and shakes his head unsympathetically.

"Empty threats …"

Logan's thick index finger lingers over the keypad and hits the command key. He stares ahead and watches as the anti-poaching cannon mounted on the bed of the jeep hums to life and blasts its lethal load of lightning-burst gunfire. Roosevelt and Butch watch in astonishment as Logan's eyes gleam with delight and a greedy smile crosses his hard features. The mercenary watches the display screen a moment for the aftermath then nods approvingly at Roosevelt.

"Impressive."

Not understanding or believing the casual cruelty just witnessed, Roosevelt attempts to speak.

"You're just a … a sickening …"

"Just a, what? It's a fine line tossing stones from where you stand, so choose your names carefully."

Logan glances around the remote location and listens to the faint but constant pop of gunfire in the distance.

"What's the range on this thing? A few miles?"
Roosevelt is silently bewildered by Logan's audacity.

"Do you actually think I would help you?"

"No? That's alright by me ... I'll just include you along with the hefty price tag and let them work it out."

The mercenary hunter stares down at the visuals on the screen and observes the aerial perspective of the unsuspecting victims of carnage.

"How long can that thing fly up there?"

"You won't get your hands on it."

"What goes up must come down and I'll find it."
Logan grins at her and maneuvers his fingers across the touchpad adjusting the drone view. Roosevelt swallows the lump in her throat as he tinkers with the controls.

"You won't find anyone to operate it for you."

"No need, I have you. Get in the jeep."
She reluctantly backs up a few steps and stands along the passenger side of the weaponized jeep.

Logan folds the computer under his arm and steps up to Butch. The two poachers follow with their automatic rifles pointed directly at the wounded safari man leaned on the vehicle. Logan offers a kindly grin and looks sympathetic at Butch's bleeding arm wound.

"Long time no see, ol' chap. I figured you'd still be around. Was that you in the chopper back there?"
Butch glares, trying to mask the pain from his wound.

"If I'd a known you was there, I would've done things so we wouldn't be having this conversation."

"Still holding onto that grudge for Tusk?"

Simultaneously both men, as if having the same thought, gaze down at Butch's clutched firearm as his aim rises slightly with a steady grip. Logan shakes his head knowingly.

"You know that won't help anyone."

Butch ponders a moment then grits his teeth and tosses the sidearm away. Logan nods his approval.

"Good, now get up front and drive."

Roosevelt stands across the jeep and watches Butch clutch her neckerchief to his bloody arm.

"He can't drive, he's wounded."

Logan turns to Roosevelt and ushers her to the jeep.

"You want to medic him some?"

"I'm not really that kind of medical doctor."

The mercenary hunter gives her a smiling wink.

"He'll do just fine. Better 'n being dead."

Butch slides into the driver's seat and Roosevelt starts to climb in next to him on the passenger side. Logan picks up his rifle, aims it at her and gestures to the rear bench alongside the anti-poaching weapon.

"You hop in back with me, Dearie."

She glares at him then crawls over the front chair to the bench alongside the assembled gear. One of the tribesmen sits in the passenger seat next to Butch and pushes his rifle barrel into the reluctant driver's ribcage. Butch stares hard at the slight framed native and the man eases the gun off to a comfortable distance.

Logan ushers the other crewman to the rear bumper while he climbs into the back and sits alongside Roosevelt. A thought crosses Logan's features and he taps Butch on the shoulder with the computer.

"I almost forgot to ask. Where's Mogambo?"
Resting his bloody hand on the steering wheel, Butch turns the ignition key and starts the open-top vehicle.

"He's gone … run off."
Logan snorts disbelievingly.

"Hardly."

The mercenary hunter lays his rifle aside, puts the computer to his lap and draws his sidearm. He cocks the piece and pulls Roosevelt close to bury the muzzle underneath her breast.

"Anything funny happens and she's dead."
A cold feeling of anguish covers Roosevelt as she speaks.

"What will your boss have to say about you killing your own men just now?"

"I'll tell him it was you. Who would say anything to the contrary?"

Roosevelt looks to the two henchmen on the jeep with their grim features and military style weapons.

"What about them?"
Logan grunts and pushes his whiskered chin in her neck.

"Their primitive minds could never comprehend what happened. They just figure its white-man magic.
Logan elbows ahead to Butch's shoulder.

"Other than war, all they know is sex, money and rock 'nd roll. Ain't that right Butchie?"

Butch lifts his foot from the clutch and grinds the shifter into low gear. The jeep lurches forward and he turns the steering wheel toward the sound of gunfire. The native crewman clinging at the back of the vehicle falls off and he hurriedly runs to leap onto his position at the rear bumper as the jeep drives away.

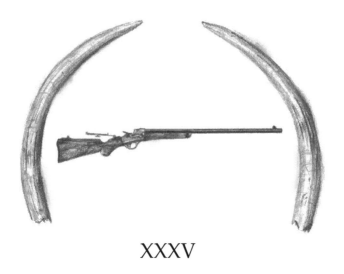

XXXV

The lumbering roar of chain-saws working against bone and flesh echoes across the moist valley floor. Tusk watches helpless as the poacher harvesting crew moves in to extract the ivory from several downed elephants. The flagrant destruction of innocent wildlife and the primordial cries of lingering death bring a tear of sorrow to the most hardened soul.

Concealed by a low dip in the terrain, Tusk creeps through the trampled grass along the edges of the heaped carnage. Through a partly obstructed view, he watches machine-gun toting poachers continuing to fire automatic rifles on bullet-riddled clusters of wounded mothers and young calves with very little ivory. The majestic beasts' screams of pain and roaring trumpets of death pierce straight to the heart of the professional white hunter.

Africa Tusk

Tusk shoulders his rifle, takes careful aim and fires the long gun. In the distance, across the marsh, a machine gun wielding poacher reels back from the lethal bullet hit and splays out on the ground. The other plunderers halt their gunfire momentarily and split off to take cover. Blinking to clear his vision, Tusk's pupils glisten with moisture which wells up at the corner of his eyes and streams down his dirt-smeared features.

The dead mountains of ivory wielding beasts strewn about the watering hole haunt his soul as the gunshots still ring in his ears.

"This has got to stop ... I have to kill Hang."
Reloading the single shot rifle, Tusk takes another shot at a poacher hiding behind the trucks before disappearing into the undergrowth.

The wreckage of the stampede-trampled campsite is mostly stashed and a large pile of freshly harvested ivory is piled and tagged. Su Long Hang paces the site making sure to supervise each bundle of ivory so that it is properly labeled for a specific trafficked destination. He draws his cell phone and snaps a few photos before tapping away at a text message.

The evening sky shines bright on the brink of an orange and purple sunset. Su Long Hang peers up from his phone to enjoy the calming view and pulls a stout, brown leafed cigar from his jacket. He clips the twisted end and clenches the rolled tobacco in his teeth before producing from another pocket an engraved zippo lighter displaying the image of a great tusker.

Eric H. Heisner

A quick flick of the flint raises a long flame and Hang passes the tip of the tobacco over the lighter. The rolled end slowly warms then glows to a burning red. Several deep puffs on the cigar put a relaxed calm into the businessman's shoulders and he marches off for a final inspection of the harvested resources.

The camp is disassembled with gear that wasn't ravaged by the stampede stowed away in the trucks. Scattered remains of cluttered garbage and a general disregard for a tidy site are left behind. Su Long Hang strolls through the campsite with the cigar protruding from his mouth and notices the general shorthandedness of the crew. He sucks on the fat wand of rolled tobacco, blows out in short puffs and shrugs off the missing members as the price of doing business.

On the horizon as the sun begins to dip below the flat-topped foliage, more than a dozen shaded mounds of slain elephants can be seen huddled around the massacre site where the animals made their final stand. Workers continue to chop at the smallest pieces of ivory including the milk teeth from the younger members of the herd. Su Long Hang stands looking out at the distant field of slaughtered carcasses and continues to smoke his cigar contently.

The sound of a familiar vintage jeep catches his ear as the whine of shifting gears grows in the distance. Hang turns his attention and watches as the post-war vehicle approaches with a trailing of dust rising up into the golden hour of sunset. He gives a short puff of the cigar and pats the concealed firearm tucked in the shoulder holster under his jacket.

Africa Tusk

The Willys Jeep bounds toward the departing poacher camp with Butch at the driver's wheel. The military style trucks are lined up readying to depart while several native crewmen hustle between stacked piles of ivory. At the sight of the gruesome display of tusks, Butch instinctively reaches for the absent firearm at his side. Logan taps his heavy boot against the back of Butch's seat and nods toward the small statured man standing at the edge of camp.

"Easy there, Butchie. Pull up, short of camp."

Logan squeezes Roosevelt close, rests his chin on her shoulder and peers down at her computer screen.

"You know which targets to select?"
She moves her hand over the touchpad and watches as the drone overhead surveys the darkening area.

"If it gets any darker, the targets won't lock."
The barrel of the pistol pushes hard into her ribcage and she groans reflexively. Logan whispers close to her ear.

"Then you best hurry up about it … like your lives depended on it."

Roosevelt types an arming code and the camera locks in on a target with a flashing red display.

"Okay, the first one is locked."

"Good … do it."

"Now?"

"Don't test me woman …"
Logan thrusts the blunt muzzle of his pistol harder into her upper ribcage and she gets the indisputable message. Roosevelt engages the firing code and the anti-poaching weapon before them hums with life.

At the near perimeter of the former encampment, Su Long Hang stands gripping his cigar at chest level, backed by an armed escort of native tribesmen. They all watch with piqued interest the strange silhouette of the burdened vehicle halted a short ways from their location. Hang squints into the shadowed horizon beneath the glow of evening sky and motions his men to follow behind as he takes a measured step closer.

The area temporarily flashes brighter as the anti-poaching cannon blazes to life and spits fire into the sky. The cigar falls from his clenched fist as the candescent light shines off Hang's dark pupils. The look of astonishment is slowly replaced by a mien of uncertain panic. Within seconds, a blast is heard from camp and Su Long Hang turns to see one of his ivory smuggling trucks explode in a mushroom cloud of flames.

Perched in back of the jeep, Peter Logan smiles with amusement at the fiery results. His chiseled features glow in the bursting light from the exploded wreckage in the distance.

"Excellent, now lock in on the others."

Roosevelt looks down at the computer monitor and half the screen is nearly masked by the bright burning blur of flaming light. She redirects the camera on the drone to gain perspective and the whole area comes into view.

Logan glances down at the screen, sees their current position at the jeep and pulls her tighter.

"Don't get any funny ideas, Doctor."

She wiggles some breathing room from Logan's embrace and resumes typing commands into the computer. Logan watches a moment, satisfied, then swings his legs over the side and stands behind her alongside the jeep.

"Tell me when you have it set up."

The faint clicking of computer keys continues another moment as Roosevelt peeks over to make eye contact with Butch in the seat ahead. She turns to Logan behind her, who watches the fading firelight on the ivory truck, and nods.

"Okay, I got it."

Logan takes the laptop computer from her hands, looks at the screen a quick second then at Butch. His dark glistening eyes squint suspiciously.

"Don't you try to cross me, understand?"

Logan jerks the female doctor backward from the rear jeep bench and puts her on the ground next to him. Roosevelt struggles to regain her feet and tries to push away from him. The unyielding mercenary hunter grips her shoulder tightly with his gun hand and lays the cold metal barrel up against her cheek.

"It's time to go to work, Doctor."

He thrusts the open computer back into her hands and escorts her toward Su Long Hang and the men standing before the flaming wreckage of vehicle.

XXXVI

The blaze of the exploded ivory truck lights up the evening sky with orange flickers of light. The burning mass behind him, Su Long Hang draws his pistol from his shoulder holster and glares toward the dark figures at the weaponized jeep. Murderous intentions fill his slanted eyes as he watches the shadowed forms move forward toward the reaches of firelight. Hang calls out as the two unknown rivals advance.

"Who the hell are you ...?"

The dimly lit pair walks into the fiery glow of the fading explosion and Hang barks angrily.

"Logan ... you cheap gun for hire, why the hell did you let her explode one of my supply trucks?"

Logan continues a few steps closer with his gun pressed into Roosevelt's side and her body pushed ahead of his.

The rolling glint of truck flames in the near background reflects off his stern features.

"I gave you a taste of why I ain't *cheap* anymore."

Su Long Hang gazes down at the remains of his glowing cigar on the ground and steps the toe of his shoe onto it. He twists the burning stub into the dirt with a last puff of smoke and contemplates Logan's strategic play at renegotiation.

"Is that the mysterious weapon?"

"It is."

Hang moves his finger inside the trigger guard on the pistol as it dangles by his side.

"I see it is quite operational."

"That's right. Successfully field tested too."

Su Long Hang's pistol hand twitches at his side.

"And she comes included with your price?"

"Correct."

The two former colleagues silently stare at each other for a long tense moment. Su Long Hang nods and slowly raises his pistol to tuck it back into the shoulder holster concealed inside his jacket. He draws out his phone and the screen powers on, glowing bright on his thin-lipped features. He swipes several commands on the electronic device and glimpses up at Logan.

"How much is it that you want?"

"Ten times what you paid me last time?"

The Chinese businessman taps a series of digits on the phone pad and holds the glowing screen faced out toward Logan.

"Done. You may now hand her over."

Logan releases his grip on Roosevelt and steps forward to read the numbers on the handheld, lighted screen. He stares at what he hopes to be a bank account transfer and reads the short message:

"EAT SHIT - YOU TRAITOR!"

The hired mercenary looks up with dismay and is greeted with Su Long Hang's pistol again in hand and pointed directly into his face. Logan falters, taking a step back in a state of angry shock and grunts.

"You dirty son of a bitch ..."

The Chinese businessman shakes his head slowly and wags the aimed pistol. Logan gets the intended message and freezes in his tracks as Hang greedily licks his lips before speaking.

"I already paid you once for a job you haven't finished yet. My policy is not to renegotiate with hired professionals or defectors."

Behind Logan, Roosevelt takes the opportunity to rouse the handheld computer with a blaze of fingertips across the touchpad. She moves a step backward and raises her voice to the men before her.

"This would be the time to start renegotiating." Logan sidesteps Hang's line of fire and the three hold their positions while staring at one another.

The mercenary hunter looks down at the barrel of Hang's handgun and they both look over to Roosevelt with her fingers poised over the laptop touchpad. Hang breaks the silence of the standoff first.

"Do you have something to contribute, Doctor?"

"The targets are locked."

Hang looks behind them at the burning truck.

Africa Tusk

"You already destroyed a quarter of my ivory."
Logan silently watches as Hang continues.

"What is your next target?"

"It would be best for us if you didn't find out."

Su Long Hang heaves a sigh and shakes his head bemused after glancing at Logan.

"You want to negotiate too. What do *you* want?"
Roosevelt keeps her fingers over the touchpad and backs another step slowly away from the two.

"Just for us all to walk away from this."
The irritated businessman raises his gun higher and turns his aim from Logan to Roosevelt.

"And how far do you think you would get?"

There is a muted, but distinct click of an old fashioned rifle hammer being cocked back just outside of the circle of firelight. The familiar voice of Tusk comes from the dim surroundings.

"She'll get a lot farther than you'd think."
Logan utters a curse under his breath and Hang turns to the glow of evening sunset and grunts his frustration.

"The infamous Tusk, I presume?"

The armed poachers supporting Hang direct their automatic rifles in the general vicinity of the new guest to the party as Tusk calls out from the dusky twilight.

"Everyone just needs to start backing away!"
The standoff remains unmoved as the combatants try to adjust their eyesight past the light of the burning vehicle. Su Long Hang turns his pistol to aim at Logan's head.

"Don't you even think of stepping away."

Logan peers into the barrel of Hang's pistol and stands firm as he continues to scan the coming nightfall.

The mercenary hunter looks to his men by the jeep with Butch and calls into the darkness.

"Tusk … I have your pal Butch over yonder. Give it up or this won't end well for anyone."

The soft crunching footfalls of boots on dry grass approach and Tusk walks into the glowing firelight of the smoldering truck. He holds the long-range hunting rifle tucked at his shoulder and turns the heavy barrel to point directly at Su Long Hang.

"We're all going to leave here … except you."
The iron sights of the single shot buffalo gun stay on the Chinese businessman as he stands and utters a reply.

"Mister Tusk, you only have one shot."

"That's all I need to do what needs doing."

The seconds pass as the armed standoff seems at an impasse. Hang's raised gun arm begins to quiver slightly and Logan notices the obvious shiver of nerves as he stares down the barrel of his former employer's weapon. A flash of firelight illuminates the night as the contents in the back of the support vehicle crumbles in a flaming pile of destruction. The singed-hair odor from the burning ivory is foul and unpleasant to the senses.

Suddenly, with a quick decisive move, Logan swings his arm out and knocks Hang's aim away from the direction of his face.

"The hell with this!"
Su Long Hang's firearm inadvertently discharges and the surprise gunshot smashes into the lighted screen of Roosevelt's computer. The electronic device tumbles from her hands and she stands in numbed shock, not knowing if she has been injured.

Africa Tusk

Tusk turns his rifle aim a few inches aside of Hang and fires the large caliber, long gun at the first tribesman to discharge his weapon into the skirmish. He quickly breaks open the breach and reloads the single shot weapon while calling out to the lady doctor.

"Run, dammit!"

Roosevelt instinctively dives for the grounded laptop and flips over the wreckage of electronics. She grabs it up as Tusk takes hold of her arm, pulling her away from the ensuing hostile gunfire.

Su Long Hang shoots off several shots at Tusk and screams at the top of his lungs.

"Shoot them damn you ... Kill them all!"

Tusk and Roosevelt dash into the dim cover of nightfall. She pulls away from him as he angles toward the weapon-bearing jeep and looks down at her bullet damaged computer, pausing momentarily. Tusk stops and urgently turns toward her.

"What are you doing now?"

Quick successive muzzle-flashes of a double rifle shoot from the shadowed trees and a pair of machine-gun firing poachers, following in pursuit, tumble to the ground. A look of divine inspiration strikes Roosevelt momentarily and she calls out blindly into the night.

"Mogambo!!"

She puts two fingers to her lips and gives out a shrill whistle that mimics Mogambo's call to warning. She stabs a finger to the command key on the computer and tosses it to the ground as Tusk shouts at her.

"C'mon, let's go!"

Eric H. Heisner

The Remington Rolling Block rifle spews a long-flaming flash from the end of the muzzle as Tusk directs another gunshot toward Su Long Hang. The targeted Chinaman luckily steps aside at the opportune moment and the tribesman standing behind him catches the large caliber bullet in the throat. Tusk reloads his long gun, glances to the damaged computer on the ground and grabs Roosevelt around the waist, pulling her to safety.

"What did you do ...?"

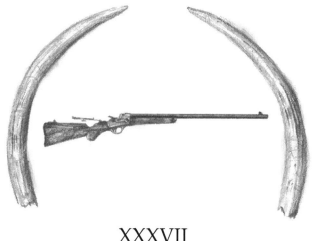

XXXVII

Gunshots explode all around and the muzzle flashes of automatic rifles light up the night. Beside the jeep, Butch hears the shrill whistle of warning and observes the two armed gunmen standing alongside him. They have their rifles tucked at their shoulder and look around confused in the looming darkness as to where they should aim their firearms. Butch turns and looks behind at the anti-poaching cannon in the jeep as it hums to life and blasts several explosive charges upward.

Temporarily blinded, his pupils narrow and his eyes go wide as he looks at the vertical trajectory pointed straight up into the sky from the condemned jeep.

"Holy shit ... she gone and done it!"

Butch hastily tosses the ignition key rattling across the jeep's hood, getting the two gunmen's attention and gives them a shove toward the unmanned vehicle.

"Time for me to go boys ..."

He tumbles away from the distracted guards and hits the ground running as the Willys Jeep receives the returning bursts of rapid cannon fire. The vehicle explodes in a flashing blue light of destroyed electronics followed by a fantastic ball of flames rising to the greyish heavens.

The mix of explosions and gunfire fill the dusk with a confused state of firelight and blackness. Tusk and Roosevelt disappear into the twilight leaving Su Long Hang standing empty-handed amongst the twin beacons of fiery wreckage. The Chinese businessman turns on his heels and marches back toward his waiting Mercedes SUV as his armed escort continues to rake the surrounding darkness with bursts from automatic rifles. The vehicle door slams shut and the reflection of firelight glimmers off the dark tinted windows.

The faint light of morning puts a purple hue to the dark horizon as several booted feet trod across the wide expanse of unmolested landscape. Roosevelt picks up her pace to keep on Tusk's heels while Butch follows in the rear. The three fugitives appear weary from the activity of the previous days and all-night trek.

Ahead in the lead, Tusk pauses and turns to gaze around. With his long rifle perched over his shoulder, barrel forward in an Africa carry, he stares to their back trail and listens intently for any hint of pursuit. Butch turns to peer back as well, studies the natural sounds and nods his head reaffirming.

"I don't hear anyone following."

Tusk returns the nod toward Butch and bows his head.

"What a damned waste…"

Roosevelt wipes the sweat from her face as she reflects on the last few hours and evening prior.

"What … my gear?"

"No, not killing Hang."

She shakes her head perturbed.

"I should hold you responsible."

"For saving your life?"

"No … for destroying my research equipment."

"I thought you said it was priceless."

Roosevelt sneers at Tusk's cavalier attitude regarding her experimental gear.

"Irreplaceable is more like it."

"Like my jeep?"

He turns his attention from their back-trail and sees that his sarcastic comments have begun to highly irritate Roosevelt. A slight smile cracks through his features and he shrugs nonchalant.

"You're the one who pushed the button."

He turns forward and gives a dejected shake his head.

"I sure wish you hadn't blown up that jeep."

Roosevelt heaves a heavy sigh, watching him start to walk away, knowing she won't get either an offer of compensation or an apology.

"Was it worth one point two million?"

Tusk puts his finger midair miming the mathematical calculation as he hikes away. He turns and calls out to Roosevelt over his shoulder.

"Hundreds of dollars at least, it was a *classic*."

"Well, I have to answer to an International Board of Directors and you just have to go down to the local junk yard to find yourself another."

He pauses a moment considering a retort then adjusts the heavy weight of the rifle on his shoulder. Without looking back he continues the walk to the river.

"Good luck to you then."

They hike a few long silent minutes until Butch coughs and waves ahead. Roosevelt and Tusk turn to their oversized, excited safari companion as he calls out.

"Hey, lookee there!"

Ahead at the river, sitting on his haunches with a rifle resting across his lap sits Mogambo. He nods at the sight of them and waits while they quicken their step.

As the three battle-worn escapees approach on foot, Mogambo stands and greets them with a broad welcoming smile. Butch is the first to clasp Mogambo's hand and give him a slap across the shoulder.

"What are you smiling at you skinny sonofa …?"

The trusted gun bearer and tracker nods agreeable and remains smiling as Butch continues to speak.

"Ya followed ahead of us to where we hadn't even gotten to yet."

Tusk stands before his loyal friend and reaches out to shake his hand. Mogambo puts his arms around Tusk, hugging him with a brotherly embrace. The white hunter looks over the trusted native and observes that he appears mostly unharmed and in good spirits.

"How'd you leave them?"

"Them Diggers in bad shape, Bwana."

"You take out their trucks?"

Mogambo nods with a reassuring grin.

"All broke down. Anythin' come out be on foot."

The thought of the smugglers getting another haul of ivory is upsetting but unavoidable. Tusk nods solemnly and pats Mogambo on the shoulder.

"We'll have a run-in with them again someday." Roosevelt gives a smile to Mogambo and turns to Tusk.

"You mean they're not put out of business?"

"Not even close. These last few days have just been a few red numbers in their accounting books." Butch steps over and gives Roosevelt a friendly nudge with his hip.

"Doesn't matter if it's Chung, Hang, Chin or someone else really, they all need to be put to a stop."

The worn down and dirt-smeared lady doctor stares at the three men before her and her jaw gapes open in disbelief.

"And you crazy blokes think you can do it all by yourselves, one at a time with your primitive methods? Tusk wrinkles his brow at her.

"Since there aren't many valid options available, it's our small contribution and has been working so far." Roosevelt gestures around them at their obvious meager existence and lack of support or supplies in the middle of the African savannah.

"Does it play out this well every time?"

The insinuation at being incompetent settles home and Tusk jabs an accusing finger in her direction.

"You're the one who destroyed our transport." Butch puts his arm around Roosevelt and speaks up.

Eric H. Heisner

"Usually, we're not up against more'n a few men, not an army with a chopper."

The native scout looks past the sociable gathering and a look of consternation comes over him.

"Bwana, you expect'n company?"

Tusk turns and follows Mogambo's line of sight. In the far distance, a trailing dust cloud whirling on the horizon can be seen from a small convoy of approaching vehicles. Butch smoothes his sweaty hair and grunts.

"All broke down, huh?"

Mogambo turns to Butch and shrugs innocently.

"Different trucks, maybe?"

Heaving his long gun up to the crook of his arm, Tusk jumps to action and ushers them toward the river.

"No time to discuss the makes and models."

The three safari men exchange a knowing glance and prepare to resume as Tusk continues.

"They'll most likely be here within the hour and we need to get to the other side of this waterway."

He ushers Roosevelt downriver toward the location of the Burma Bridge and the others follow along.

The four weary travelers jog down the riverbank as multiple crocodiles scamper along the grassy shore and sidle into the rushing muddy waters. Butch watches the prehistoric creatures and makes an audible gulping sound. Ahead, a small grouping of Thomson gazelle darts from the edges of the disturbed watercourse.

Roosevelt looks to the faraway haze of vehicle dust rising skyward and shakes her head disbelievingly.

"How did they get resupplied so fast?"

Africa Tusk

The dense, waist-high grasslands along the river's edge are unnerving with their hidden contents and Tusk keeps his rifle cocked and ready.

"Really doesn't matter how or why. We're in no condition to receive unwanted visitors."
He puts a supportive hand to the top of her backside and urges her forward.

"We need to pick up the pace and find that bridge if we hope to find cover on the other side before they make the crossing."

XXXVIII

A rifle fastened over his shoulder, Mogambo works his way across the primitive bridge which simply consists of three suspended ropes. In the water below, several log-like river predators pass by attentively. Their large reptilian eyes protrude from the water's surface as they swish long tails against the current in anticipation of a meal opportunity. Mogambo reaches the opposite shore and unslings his rifle to hold at the ready.

The sagging bridge sways in the breeze and Tusk ushers Roosevelt forward, holding the lines steady.

"You're next Doc, get to it."

The aged ropes tense under her weight and she begins to slink her way across. As Roosevelt nears the center-point of the river, the single line at the bottom sags into the water and the current flows over the toe of her boots.

Africa Tusk

Tusk and Mogambo meet each other's gaze as they keep fingers firm on triggers. Tusk clenches his jaw and waits patient with the rifle nested against the hollow of his shoulder. On opposite shores, the watchful figures scan the river's surface ready to deter a potential feeding attack from the rushing current.

Mogambo lowers the tip of his rifle and calls out a quiet warning to Roosevelt.

"Memsahib, hold'n high line 'nd keep feet dry." Roosevelt tucks her elbows and supports more weight with her arms causing the lower foot line to rise from the flowing waterway. Butch timidly eyes the twisted fibers of creaking rope stretched taut over dangerous waters.

"Tusk ol' pal, you can go next. I'll wait here."

The focused marksman keeps silent as he watches Roosevelt progress past the perilous midpoint. He takes his eyes from the rushing water a moment as he glances back at the visible dust trail of approaching vehicles and looks to Butch questioningly.

"What were you saying, Butchie?"

"I said I ain't gonna step on that thing." Tusk turns back to the crossing as Roosevelt nears the opposite shore and he looks down to the passing current.

"You'd rather swim it?"

Butch heaves an unenthusiastic snort as he watches another vigorous river crocodile slither through the grass on the shore and flop into the muddy stream.

"You think'n to protect me from them beasties?" Tusk nods with a shrug.

"I'll sure try."

"Ha, horseshit! Not good enough. You and that damned single-shot ain't gonna reload fast enough for me. I'd rather find a hole 'nd hide out for a week while I build a boat or an airplane."

Tusk looks to the telling dust indications of the nearing trucks and tilts his head negative.

"That's not an option unfortunately. We don't have the supplies to hang around here. You'll get yer rump across that bridge and we'll hold them off from the far side of the river."

"That ain't any sort of a bridge to me and we don't know how many there are coming behind."

"If they get detained in the crossing, it won't matter. We'll keep them there till dark then slip away.

On the opposite shore, Roosevelt leaps from the ropes to the riverbank and waves. Tusk lowers his rifle and ushers a hand toward the Burma Bridge.

"You're up, pard."

The burly safari man bows and gestures mockingly in return for Tusk to hit the waiting ropes.

"After you, Bwana."

"Dammit Butch, we don't have time to argue!"

Butch stares at Tusk a long moment and like a pouty child, shuffles his feet forward until he reaches up to take a firm hold of the higher lines. He heaves his weight on the twisted twine fibers and casts a doubting look toward Tusk.

"This is crap, I tell ya."

One boot steps up on the lower line followed by the other and Butch's large frame gyrates and sways with the movement of the three individually hung ropes.

Africa Tusk

The burly man cautiously works his way across until he nears the middle where his feet weigh the ropes down into the passing current. He looks back at Tusk who holds his rifle firmly to his shoulder, ready to fire. Disgruntled, he shakes his head at his old friend.

"This bridge is bullshit!"

A long slender head and protruding eyes of a river crocodile swims near and Tusk puts a shot into the water, just grazing its snout. It quickly spins with a splash and dives underwater as Butch pulls his feet up clear of the current.

"What the hell was that?"

Tusk lowers the rifle, opens the breach and reloads.

"I missed."

"What the hell do you mean, you missed?"

"Dammit Butch, don't stop there with your knees all wet and yer mouth hanging open ... keep moving."

The oversized man in khaki lowers his chin and resumes the progression, making the rope lines creak with every shift of his weight.

A recoiling snap echoes across the river crossing and the foot rope suddenly shudders away from the lowest point and goes limp into the flowing current. The broken line snakes to the water's surface leaving the safari hunter dangling from both his handholds. Butch hangs knee deep in the river and cranes his head back at Tusk with an expression of suspected culpability.

A sudden splash of water is heard as a crocodile lunges forward and is quickly intercepted by a gunshot from Mogambo's rifle. The lethal projectile smashes into the exposed head and flips the long reptile belly up.

Twitching, the animal lies prone in the water a moment before other aquatic inhabitants catch the trace of blood and lunge in to clean up the kill. Knees held high and eyes bugged wide, Butch quickly crosses the distance to shore like an oversized ape, swinging hand over hand.

Roosevelt stands alongside Mogambo and watches as Tusk turns his attention from Butch to the rising fantail of dust from the approaching vehicles. She lets her eyes fall to the bridge's lower rope as it leads downstream in separate pieces from opposite shores. Her gaze travels to Tusk as he gives a curt wave before shouldering his rifle and dissolving back into the brush.

"Hey, wait a minute!"

Butch leaps to the embankment and scampers a safe distance from the river's edge before looking to the opposite shore. The opposing riverbank is vacant; Tusk is gone and only the intact bridge pieces remain.

"Where did he go?"

Roosevelt shakes her head disbelievingly.

"He just waved and disappeared."

Shrugging his shoulders in disgust, Butch turns to Mogambo who nods in agreement. They look to the far riverbank and Butch snorts toward Roosevelt.

"Alright, let's move out."

The confused female stands watching across the muddy waters, waiting for something to happen.

"What about Tusk?"

"He'll just do what he does."

Her eyes lift to the hint of track haze from the approaching vehicles, rising above the scrubby tree-line.

Africa Tusk

The faint engine murmur of the convoy can be heard traveling in the gentle breeze.

"We can't leave him over there."

"He's the one who left us. Now come on."

He takes her arm and pulls her along a few steps. She holds back and stares at the dangerous crossing of the flowing river.

"What's he going to do?"

Butch gestures for Mogambo to continue along and turns to the concerned lady doctor whose survival is now his responsibility.

"He'll keep 'em from crossing that river."

Roosevelt watches for any activity across the waterway and Butch gently gives her a tug on the sleeve.

"C'mon, we have to go ..."

She turns hesitantly a last time to murmur a heartfelt goodbye then moves away from the water's edge to follow behind Butch and Mogambo.

XXXIX

Hidden in the tall tangle of grass near the river crossing, Tusk squats in the stifling heat and waits for the looming approach of vehicles. The sweat pours into his eyes as he squints into the distance and studies the dust covered details of the shrouded trucks. They continue to drive nearer, heading for the gravel shoaled river crossing at a direct and decidedly unhurried pace.

Rifle rested across his thigh, Tusk adjusts the long range Creedmoor sights, slowly and methodically. He checks the cartridge loaded in the rifle and makes a count of the remaining few finger-sized, soft point loads in his ammo belt. The rattling rumble of military truck frames on the uneven path continues to approach and Tusk raises the rifle to his shoulder.

Africa Tusk

On the far side of the waterway, Mogambo guides the others along a wide trampled animal track, high on the riverbank. He hesitates then signals for them all to stop and bend low in the grass. The native guide's bright eyes roll in their sockets scanning while the rest of his lithe frame crouches in stillness. Paused in the hot brush, Roosevelt whispers to Butch kneeling beside her.

"What are we doing?"

Butch puts his hand up and motions for silence. A scampering rushing sound rustles through the thick underbrush and Mogambo stays frozen in his tracks with the rifle held ready. Roosevelt loses the color in her flushed features and rasps toward Butch.

"What is it?"

"Hush now!"

A guttural roar erupts from the wavering thicket as a nine foot crocodile races at them. Mogambo deftly aims and fires two quick shots into the wide, gaping jaws of the charging beast. Butch hastily jerks Roosevelt aside and Mogambo leaps high in the air as the dead reptilian form continues its swift momentum and slides toward them.

Her eyes wide with horror, Roosevelt looks down at the massive prehistoric looking creature as Mogambo straddles the kill. He thrusts his knife blade, deep into the animal, just above its neck along the spine. A stream of blood oozes from the mouth as the long white teeth form a deadly row of protruding choppers. She turns to Butch who merely smiles coolly and winks.

"If we had time Missy, I'd make boots."

Ears perked to the quick succession of two popping gunshots from the direction of the river, Tusk watches as the advancing trucks suddenly halt and the trailing dust passes over. Peering down along the iron sights, he stares ahead disbelievingly and utters aloud.

"Huh … surprised to see you here."

Tusk lowers the rifle and stands from his concealed spot.

Eyes squinted to the western horizon, he watches as a lone figure exits the passenger door and stands in front of the dark silhouetted vehicles. The quiet idling rumble of engines across the grassy plain is the only sound as Tusk puts a hand up to his brow to shade his gaze. With his rifle held at his side, he walks toward the waiting individual standing in front of the trucks.

Mogambo trots ahead, moving quickly across the shorter dry grasses away from the waterway. He leads Butch and Roosevelt to a secluded, tree shrouded hiding spot within watching distance of the shallower section of riverbed. The native safari scout crouches down in the thorny brush and gestures for the others to do the same.

"Good spot for waiting, here."

Butch pulls a thorny bramble from his sleeve and looks out toward the gravel shoals of the crossing.

"Is there any sight of him?"

Mogambo shakes his head slightly as his gaze scans the area. Roosevelt squats low and watches the distant riverbank for any signal from Tusk. The forthcoming cloud of dust in the air has now dissipated into the hazy afternoon firmament.

Africa Tusk

The blazing sun nearing the horizon begins to dip behind the trees along the riverbank and the golden light of afternoon glints in their eyes. Roosevelt looks over at her travel companions as they sit waiting patiently.

"Shouldn't we get some distance from them?" Butch leans close and speaks quietly.

"This is a good place to hide and see what'll turn out. I want to know what our ol' pal has in mind and it's better to have an idea of where they are before dark than to try 'nd outrun them a' foot."

The faint rumble of several engines is heard after another short spell of waiting and the source of the track haze comes into view. All three watch from cover as the dark dusty vehicles pause at the riverbank then slowly ease into the moving waterway which rushes up over the wheel wells. Butch looks questioningly at Mogambo who hugs the double rifle and offers a naïve shrug.

The dark, dusty military Rovers rumble across the shallow crossing and begin to rise up on the other side dripping water from the windows down. Roosevelt clears her throat and whispers hoarsely toward the two men at her side.

"I thought the plan was to somehow stop and keep them from crossing that river?"

"Yeah …"

Butch stares at the trucks breaching the shore and puts his hand on his mouth to scratch his whiskered cheek.

"Well … he either changed the plan or he'll be passing as croc dung in a day or so."

Roosevelt stares at Butch, horrified and he turns to her.

"Sorry Missy, but it's a definite possibility. We'll do our best to stay hidden and let them pass us by."

The three fugitives observe from concealment as the dark SUVs trailed by military supply trucks each crawl up on the near riverbank then drive away from the shallow crossing toward them. The slow procession seems to be steering directly at their hiding spot and Roosevelt begins to show concern. She tilts her gaze down toward Butch's lap as he quietly draws his knife and holds it firmly in hand.

"How long are we going to wait here?"
He carefully watches the truck convoy's approach.

"Until they pass or they find us, I guess."

"That's not really a plan."

"No? More of a wait 'n see reaction, I guess."

The motorcade of military vehicles draws closer and wet brakes squeak to a halt several meters away. The dark heavy tint of the forward windows and the low sun shining behind conceals the occupants inside until one of the passenger doors swings slowly open. From the concealed underbrush, the three watch the emerging figure at the stopped convoy.

The extended form of a tall safari boot touches the ground and the door swings back to reveal Tusk stepping out of the lead vehicle. His squinted gaze peers curiously into the surrounding thicket of brush and he reaches into the Rover to grab his long gun from inside. Tusk cradles the rifle casually under his arm and looks the area over. He puts two fingers between his lips and blows out a shrill, signal whistle.

Africa Tusk

A flutter of winged fowl takes to flight as the passenger doors on the other military Rovers and trucks swing open. Several armed soldiers outfitted in jungle camo fatigues step out alongside a familiar-looking government official. In full dress uniform, Jimmy Franks walks to the front of the vehicle, across the wet, dripping bumper from Tusk and scans his narrowed eyes along the seemingly unoccupied brush. A wide, toothy smile appears on his features as he raises his voice to project over a far distance.

"Hello, out there … would you like a ride?"

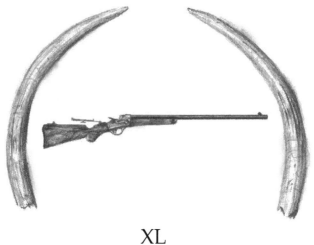

XL

The hot afternoon rays of sunlight glisten off the dark painted military vehicles and the long, trim shadows of armed soldiers extend forward to the scrubby brush line. Tusk hoists his long rifle onto his shoulder as he watches Mogambo, Roosevelt and Butch emerge from the tangled brambles of thick undergrowth. A hint of a smile crosses his lips and he offers a greeting nod as they approach.

"Glad to see you all safe."

Moving at a jaunty strut in the lead, Roosevelt is the first to speak up. She looks from the military convoy of waiting vehicles to Tusk, then gestures inquiringly toward Jimmy Franks.

"Where the heck did he come from?"

The safari hunter steps away from the front of the truck to Roosevelt and pats her kindly on the shoulder.

"Those were my thoughts exactly. On most days, I'm not too enthused to see these guys. I have a surprise for you. Come look at what he found."

Puzzled about the state of affairs, Roosevelt walks with Tusk while Mogambo and Butch curiously follow.

Opening the rear passenger door on the second Land Rover, Tusk steps back to reveal Su Long Hang perched on the bench seat with handcuffed shackles secured across his lap. The Chinese ivory smuggler looks solemn and distant as his eyes flit over at her then forward again. A series of insults mumbled in a foreign tongue escape through his lips as he sits in bondage. Roosevelt casts a probing expression toward Tusk until Jimmy Franks steps up with his broad, toothy grin.

"We were contacted by Samburu herdsmen and told of a convoy of potential poachers crossing their grazing land. The fiery wreckage of a helicopter pointed the way and it wasn't hard to follow up with the rest."

The poaching kingpin sits before her in custody and Roosevelt can hardly believe what she is witnessing. It takes a while to process the transformed circumstances with the incapacitated poacher trucks being towed behind official military vehicles. She takes a calm breath then inquiries of the government official.

"What about Logan?"

Jimmy Franks' smile fades for the moment with a shrug.

"Unfortunately, Mister Logan was absent from the scene and was nowhere to be found."

Su Long Hang glares over at the lady doctor then growls at the uniformed official.

"He better stay away or I will kill him myself!"

"You should save your breath for your lawyer."
With his enduring smile gleaming again, Jimmy Franks slams the vehicle door, blocking out Hang's presence. The prim government agent turns to face the ragtag group of civilians and lifts a curious eye.

"The question posed for me here as an official government envoy is what to do with you reprobates?"

Tusk lowers the butt-plate of his rifle stock to the ground and leans on the long steel barrel. He knits his brow and gazes around innocently.

"No paperwork needed. We were just passing through and in need of a friendly ride."
Jimmy looks from the safari hunter to the lady doctor.

"Ahh, and what of your special mission, Doctor?"
Roosevelt looks to the surrounding faces backed by the military convoy and purses her lips into a guilty smile.

"All of my special experimental equipment was unfortunately destroyed in a tragic accident while doing precision tests in the field."

Jimmy Franks pauses to think on the matter and shakes his head with a smile.

"Probably for the best, I presume. Therefore, if you have no luggage and would like a ride back to some sort of civilization, welcome aboard."
Roosevelt looks to Tusk and gives an innocent nod.

"Yes, yes I would. Thank you, Mister Franks."
Jimmy Franks offers his arm and she takes it, letting him escort her toward the lead vehicle.

With a sly hint of mockery to her voice, she queries the uniformed government official.

Africa Tusk

"Tell me ... who is this bad man you captured single handedly? I wager it is quite the exciting story."
Roosevelt winks over her shoulder at Tusk. Not one to pass on creating a good story, Jimmy Franks plays into her womanly charms.

"Oh, Doctor Adams, it is really quite fascinating. Let me tell you all about it ..."

Tusk looks at Mogambo and Butch. They all look rather amused at her wily manipulation of ego with the government official. The professional hunter hefts his rifle to his shoulder and turns to the convoy.

"I guess we ride in the back with the troopers?"

Days later, at the headquarters of the Kalispell Safari Ranch, two dusty government Land Rovers wait out front with Jimmy Franks standing near the foremost vehicle. Beneath a pair of dark sunshades he smiles while looking up to the front porch. Sheltered from the midday sun by the overhanging roofline, Roosevelt says her goodbyes to Tusk and his steadfast crew.

Roosevelt embraces Mogambo in a warm hug and grasps his hands in hers with a gesture of gratitude.

"I wanted to thank you Mogambo, for being my diligent protector and watching out for me always."
A calm breeze moves the warm air across the porch and Mogambo silently accepts her generous thanks with kind bright eyes. He steps aside as she moves over to Butch.

"How can I ever repay you, Butch?"

"Usually cash is best ... for you there is no need, was glad to have you around. Intellectual conversation with these old chaps can get awful tiresome."

Butch extends his hand and the attractive female takes it then leans in to deliver a gentle kiss to his cheek. His broad shoulders hunch around flushed features and the oversized safari guide appears to morph into a shy schoolboy in short pants. Roosevelt holds his large calloused palm and caresses it with her slender fingers.

"You're one heck of a cook and transpo man."

Butch nods and seems to almost flutter his eyes sheepish as Roosevelt moves on down the line to Tusk. Keenly observing his old pal melt from her female charms, Tusk wags his chin with an amused grimace. The white hunter extends his hand in a cool professional manner and the doctor grasps it in a firm but gentle grip.

Roosevelt peers up at Tusk, connecting with his attentive gaze and eases herself a full step closer to him. She wraps her free arm around the back of his neck and pulls him in close for a passionate kiss on the mouth. The discerning spectators watch with delight as the two travel companions seem to lose themselves in pent-up desire of the moment then just as suddenly, separate. Tusk bows his head, releases his handshake grip with her and passes a caressing hand across his wet lips.

"No words of thanks are necessary for me."

The lady doctor tosses the strands of blowing hair away from her blushed cheek and gives the coy safari hunter a sly wink.

"Keep up the good fight, Mister Kalispell."

"You as well, Doctor."

The seasoned safari crew on the porch is speechless as Roosevelt saunters down the steps and climbs into the military Land Rover parked alongside Jimmy Franks.

Africa Tusk

The government official closes the door after she enters and turns to look up at the men on the shaded veranda. Flashing his signature wide, beaming grin, Jimmy Franks waves and shouts toward them.

"Saving the best for last, I presume. I cannot wait for her passionate farewell to me!"

The cheerful uniformed agent steps around the military vehicle and climbs inside leaving the audience on the porch watching the dark tinted vehicles pull away down the dusty lane. Butch steps over and places his large paw on Tusk's shoulder. They both stare silently as the trucks drive away until Butch finally grunts.

"What a woman ..."

Tusk's eyes dart over to his old friend.

"Yeah ... let's have a drink."

Butch swipes a thick finger across his pursed lips and runs his tongue along the front of his teeth. His whiskered cheeks spread to a knowing smile as he nods.

"Yes, Bwana."

Mogambo melts away into the shadows around the side of the house and the two old friends turn to go inside.

In the central great room of the ranch house, Tusk and Butch move toward the bar setup. They both simultaneously peer up at the diminished trophy mount with fresh bullet holes in the wall behind and the horn spike trimmed away on one side. Butch grabs up a swirling liquor bottle and slaps his hand on Tusk's back with a jaunty laugh.

"*What a woman!*"

The End ...

AFRICA TUSK

AN ADVENTURE NOVEL

BY ERIC H. HEISNER

Eric H. Heisner is an award winning writer, actor and filmmaker. He is the author of several Western novels: *West to Bravo, T.H. Elkman* and *Short Western Tales: Friend of the Devil*. His adventure novel, *Wings of the Pirate* is due out in the coming year. He can be contacted at his website: www.leandogproductions.com

Ethan Julio Pro was born in 2001 to a multi-talented and creative family. Raised in Santa Clarita, California he showed an affinity for the arts at a very young age and demonstrated a natural skill well beyond his years. Continuing with his artistic gift, he aims to follow in his father's footsteps with a career as a professional artist.

T. H. Elkman

Tale of a Wandering Cowboy

A Western novel by

Eric H. Heisner

www.leandogproductions.com

WEST TO BRAVO

A Western Novel

By Eric H. Heisner

WWW.LEANDOGPRODUCTIONS.COM

Wings of the Pirate

A high-flying Adventure Novel

By Eric H. Heisner

Limited time pre-order at:

www.inkshares.com

illustrations by

Al P. Bringas

www.leandogproductions.com